PREFACE

These are my thoughts and my memories with no certain time line, as I have remembered them. My memories in my childhood are faint and filled with anxiety and abuse but I desperately need to uncover some loving memories. Surely there must be some.

As the song writer once said, "His Eye is on the Sparrow, and I know he watches me."God didn't promise us a bed of roses, but he did promise to walk with us along the way.

The Golden Rule says it best: Do unto others as you would have them do unto you.

Then John 3:16 "For God so loved the world, that he gave his only begotten Son, that whosoever believeth in him should not perish, but have everlasting life."

DEDICATION

This book is dedicated to my children:
Toby Wayne Causey
Glen David Timmons (Thomas)
Perry Jay Thomas
Joseph Michael Thomas
Zachariah James Causey

My blended family children:
Tambra Hale
Timothy Brumley
Alicia Blankenship
Amber Cates

Being a mom was one of my greatest joys.
Mom loves each and everyone of you. I truly miss
Glen, his smile and his loving spirit.

Things I cherish most is spending time with
my children. I love my grandchildren (all 13 of
them), but cherish their parents more.

THANK YOU

The following people helped greatly
to make my book what it is:
John Brumley
Glenda Clemens
Dianne Burris - Elling
Without their help and suggestions,
it wouldn't be the same.

I also want to thank all my encouragers who
pushed me to putting this down in writing.

I also want to thank my Lord and Savior for helping
me overcome the demons from my life, giving me
strength to write my story so that hopefully others
can find the joy and peace, knowing there is a brighter
tomorrow, and finding me a mate to love and cherish.

CHAPTER 1

Looking for Answers

Cia watched out the window of the pickup truck. She and her husband Jock decided to sell their home in Norman, Oklahoma and move to Oak Grove, Louisiana about ten miles from Jock's childhood home. They'd bought a travel trailer they would live in while renovating their new home, an early 20th century Craftsman home.

She smiled remembering the joy of seeing the home for the first time. Both she and her older sister had always yearned to have a Craftsman home. Now Cia's dream of such a home was coming true.

As the miles passed, she felt herself relaxing. With her husband driving, she could let her mind wander and dream of all the plans for their new forever home. Before the move, her cousin Kathryn Beasley had visited with them several times as they planned their big change of living. Cia loved becoming closer with her cousin. Now, they weren't just cousins they were friends.

Kathryn shared lots of family photos. Cia treasured getting to see pictures of their parents when they were children. Kathryn knew lots of stories about the cousins, aunts, and uncles. Most of them Cia couldn't remember. She told Kathryn, "I can't remember Grandmother's voice. I don't even remember if she ever talked to me. I remember seeing her working around the kitchen, but I don't remember her voice."

Cia wanted to remember those time. They sounded special and not at all like Cia remembered her life as a child. All she could remember seemed to be heartache and abuse. After talking with Kathryn about her memories and longing to remember what the pieces of her life were, Cia decided that one of the first things she needed to do in Oak Grove, Louisiana was to find a counselor. A neighbor suggested Sandy Carver, said she was the best in the area.

Cia called the counselor and set up her first appointment with Sandy Carver.

****

Cia sat in the waiting room in the office of Sandy Carver. The clock on the wall seemed to be ticking louder and louder the longer she sat there. She was a bit nervous but was determined to find at least a little peace in her mind and heart. She held on to the hope that counseling would help her.

"Cia?"

Cia looked up to see an attractive woman standing near her. She smiled and said, "I was wool gathering."

The woman chuckled and held out her hand. "I'm Sandy Carver. If you're ready let's go back to my office and we'll have a chat."

Cia nodded, stood up and took a deep breath, She thought, *well, here goes nothing."*

The sweet smell of Chamomile filled the room. Cia relaxed a bit. Chamomile was her favorite smell. The room was decorated with soft feminine colors and furnishings. The reason Cia chose a woman counselor was because the last time she tried going to a counselor, the counselor was a man, and all he wanted was to paw at her and make her feel uncomfortable.

Sandy asked "How can I help you Cia?

Cia explained, "I was talking with my cousin Kathryn, and I told her I can't remember anything but heartache and abuse in my childhood until the latter half of my 4th grade. I hope that I had some good times like Kathryn described. I can't remember them. What's heartbreaking is I can't even remember my grandmother's voice. We spent lots of time around her until we moved when I was in the 4th grade. I'm here, with the hope you might help me."

Sandy asked, "What would be your best outcome talking with me?"

"I hope you will help me remember and have insight. I hope I can trigger my mind to remember those special times, especially with my grandmother."

"Good," Sandy said and nodded.

Cia thought *I feel a bit better already and there's a little hope in my heart.*

Sandy continued "Have you ever written any of your experiences into a diary?"

"No, not since I was a child. My father took my diary from me and tore it to shreds. I never wrote about my feelings ever again."

Sandy said, "I will never take your diary away."

Cia nodded. "Jock my husband encouraged me to come to see you today. He wants my anxieties about my childhood eased."

"Good," Sandy said. "He sounds like he would never take your diary away."

"I'm sure he won't."

"Let's get started then. First I suggest you buy a diary to record your thoughts and feelings. Make it a pretty diary, one that you will feel proud of and more so, that you will want to pick up and write. She suggested that Cia make sure to write some each day in her diary. Find you a place where you will not be interrupted and that you enjoy. You've recently started the remodel of your home and I'm sure there are lots of places that you can sit and be able to daydream and collect your thoughts. It doesn't have to be in order, just as she remembered things, write them down. She advised her to keep the diary with her at all times.

When the session ended, Cia felt like she could accomplish this. She hoped her writing would bring happiness. If it didn't, then her memories would be true and that would be that for her childhood.

****

Cia was relieved but anxious to write. On the way home Cia went to the bookstore and searched for her diary. She found one with red and purple flowers on it and knew it was perfect. Those were her favorite colors. The pages were slightly scented with a relaxing smell of lavender. The diary felt good, was pretty and my oh my, the smell.

Cia felt light and happy. She walked across the parking lot to her car and said, "Now I'll go home, sit down and write out the thoughts that are racing through my head."

****

CHAPTER 2

Memories of Childhood

When Cia arrived at home her husband Jock was anxious to hear about her visit with the counselor. "How did it go?"

Cia said, "I really like her a lot. By the end of the session, I felt a flicker of hope. She suggested I buy a diary, a pretty one so I would love writing in it,"

Jock said, "I've found writing down my feelings has helped me a lot."

"How?"

"Well, when I write about whatever's going on it helps me to see my path more clearly and what direction I want to take next."

Cia thought, I had no idea he journaled. She grinned and felt her anxieties release.

Cia said, "Jock Lewis Bonner you continue to amaze me. It means more than you can imagine how positive your support for me is."

He grinned, "Well, Cia Snow Bonner, it's my pleasure. I want you to have your best life."

She kissed his check and said, "Thanks."

He kissed her back and nodded. "You're welcome."

Cia thought, I'm going to work hard to keep my thoughts from destroying me ever again.

****

Cia sat in the area where the screened in back porch would be. She could imagine hearing the fountains flowing, smelling the fragrance of flowers she would plant, and relished in the light breeze. She cozied into the chair with her favorite pen and new diary. She began writing.

Cia decided to write preface to the diary. She wrote these are my thoughts and my memories with no certain time line, as I have remembered them. My memories in my childhood are faint and filled with anxiety and abuse but I desperately need to uncover some loving memories. Surely there must be some.

She decided to not worry about the order of writing. She instead just started writing. She wrote:

> *The next thing I remember is the sound of brakes squealing and cars crashing together. I was flung from the backseat into the floorboard. Daddy slammed on his brakes. He had left a broken headlight in the floorboard. We were on our way to get a new one to replace it. It was 1956, before children were thought much of and protected from the ravages of being in a vehicle unrestrained. My face was bleeding. Daddy was mad because the car in front of them had suddenly stopped and he ran into the back of them. He got out and yelled at the person who was driving the car in front of us. Momma was in the front seat, pregnant with my oldest little brother. My two sisters were in the back seat with me and trying to help me, but they were young and didn't have any way to help my bleeding. I remember I thought to myself, I need help, but momma or daddy aren't helping me. When daddy came back from yelling at the lady, he was even madder to see me in the floorboard and bleeding. He ranted about I'd be scarred for the rest of my life, my beautiful face ruined. Later I remember being in the doctor office getting stitches in my face. I wasn't very old. I'm not sure exactly how old I was but probably around 4 or 5. The doctor apologized that I would have a scar on my face. From that moment for-*

ward, I believed I looked horrible. After all, my father told me my face was ruined. I remember when I got home and looked it mirror, it wasn't all that bad. As I grew the scar became smaller but to this day, I still see the scar and hear all the horrifying sounds and things that were said.

****

Cia took a deep breath, shook her head, and walked around the area where the porch would be for a bit. It was difficult to bring herself back from that trauma. She went into the trailer, poured herself a glass of ice-cold Diet Dr. Pepper and went back to the porch area, sat her drink on the folding table beside her chair, sat down and picked up her diary and pen. She wrote:

I remember being sick a lot. I had every childhood disease there was at the time. I remember I had to miss a lot of school during the first two years of school. First and second grades are a blur. I can remember the worst disease we had was German Measles. My sisters, Martha, Lizzy, and myself, all had the German measles at the same time. Mom moved us to the living room and made pallets for us to sleep on. She said it was easier for her and she could darken the room. We couldn't have any sunlight during the day. I remember it felt really strange to be in the dark in the middle of the day. There was a light in the adjacent room but nothing directly where we were. I was very sick with high fever. Momma put socks on our hands to keep us from scratching the sores. She said we would have scars from scratching so the socks went on! We tried hard not to scratch. She doctored our sores and that helped some. It was a very miserable time, but we did overcome and in a couple of weeks we were able to see our cousins and extended family again. I was relieved. I thought we might die.

****

Cia closed her diary, stood up and walked around the yard. It was a mess now with all the renovations, but she could imagine where each plant, bush, tree, and flower would be. She thought again about her childhood. She didn't want her diary to be all doom and gloom but had to dig deep for interesting and fun memories.

She went back to the porch area by the trailer, sat down and picked up her diary and pen. "Well." She told herself, "All I can come up with next is my tonsils, so I'll write about my constant sore throats and getting my tonsils out."

> *My mother told me that I was going to the hospital to have my tonsils out. She told me I would go to sleep while they took out the tonsils and then I would come home again and have all the ice cream I wanted. I was excited, because I loved ice cream. However, when I was admitted to the hospital, I began to run a temperature—again! The doctor said I would have to stay and have antibiotics and be rid of fever before they could do surgery. Surgery day finally came. Mom had to be at home with the other kids. She said, "You are 5 and you're big enough to obey your father." He worked nights and slept during the day. He told me he would be right there and would lay his head on my bed so I could wake him if I needed anything. Well, when I awoke from the surgery, I was thirsty. Daddy was asleep with his head on my bed, I didn't want to wake him. I couldn't stand to talk so I thought I'd just get up and get me a drink. Little did I know that I wouldn't be able to walk due to the medications that I had been given. When I fell daddy jumped and was really worried. He punched the nurse's button and came around to where I was. He told the nurse what had happened. I was really scared because there was lots of blood all over my gown, in the floor and now on daddy, while he was trying to help. They took me back to surgery to stop the bleeding. In my mind, I knew this was nothing like momma had said, and there was no ice cream either. I was disappointed and again afraid I might die. They brought me back to the room and I started bleeding a second time. I was scared silly. I didn't like*

the taste of blood and knew if I was bleeding, something bad was happening. The doctor told daddy he would have to take me back to surgery and cauterize the area where they had taken out the tonsils. For some reason my blood was not clotting. That worried me because I didn't know what that meant. I was told when they brought me back that if I didn't have another bleeding episode that I would be able to have a drink and ice cream afterwards. I was glad I didn't have to go to surgery again. I was certain I was going to die but finally I felt better and no more bleeding. Best of all, I got to have ice cream and go home to Momma.

CHAPTER 3

Birthday Present and Grade School

Cia fixed her Diet Dr. Pepper, got her Adkins breakfast bar and went to the area where the back screened in deck had been built, but the screens were not going to be put in until the house was farther along to keep from damaging the screens, to settle in for a few hours of writing. She had reread what she had already written and was brought to tears. She couldn't believe all this had happened to her as a child when she was barely 5 years old.

I remembered something that was supposed to be happy, but in reality, really was yet another trauma inflicted on me and my sister Martha. I remembered our father had brought home a new bicycle for my older sister Martha. She'd learned to ride a bicycle at our cousin Byron's house. He had all the neat toys and we all loved playing at his house, even though daddy didn't let us go there often. Martha rode up and down the street several times with our parents watching. There were several boys in our neighborhood who were very mean. After our parents went inside the house, the boys had a rope, stretched it across the road, one on each side of the street, and when Martha came riding through, they pulled the rope tight and caused her to crash. The handlebars hit her in the upper thigh and caused a really big knot. Later Martha had to have the knot surgically removed. Daddy gave the bicycle away. I don't remember who he gave it to but none of us had a bicycle after that. Poor Martha, her present went away as fast as she had received it. I felt so sorry for her. She of course was blamed for not watching out for the boys.

It was hard for Cia to wrap her head around the brutality

of her father. Sure, the boys caused the accident, but her father made it worse. Blaming Martha made no sense – then or now.

****

The day was beginning to heat up a bit, so Cia decided to move back into the trailer to continue writing in her diary. She found a quiet place and comfortable chair to sit in. It was a struggle to think about her childhood. Sometimes she could remember everything as if it were yesterday. Other times she couldn't remember how it felt to be a child – ever.

The next thing I remember was when my father had passed out from a shot. I had gotten the mumps. This was not long after I had had my tonsils out. Daddy had not had the mumps as a child and the doctor made a house call to give him a gamma globulin shot in hopes that he would not catch the mumps. The doctor hit a vein and daddy passed out. I was watching from my bed. I was so scared. Daddy was always so mean and bigger than life, I just couldn't imagine what had happened. I thought maybe the Lord had come to take him home, like he preached about, and I had heard in church. The doctor sat by his side until he finally awoke, 3 hours later. I didn't know if he would take it out on me. I don't remember anything other than that. Not sure what happened after this.

****

Cia's thoughts quickly went to her mom and wondered how she could let all these happen to her children. Her mother was a great cook, wonderful care giver as far as providing food and clothes for her children and a clean house for them to live in. What was lacking was the love, protection, and attention to them. As children were mainly sent outside to play. We didn't have lot of interaction with her until we were older. Cia began writing in her diary again.

I remember being covered in sores all over my body.

Something was biting me and neither the doctors nor my parents could figure it out. The bites would go all the way to the bone before starting to heal. The medicine smelled like tar. It was very uncomfortable. I was in the 3rd grade. My teacher had the boys and girls sitting every other one. When there was a visitor to the class, they were to put their heads down and rest while the teacher talked with the visitor. One day in particular, the boys were feeling their oats and started tickling all the girls. Of course, we giggled and became unruly. We embarrassed our teacher in front of the visitor and she was furious. As soon as the visitor left, she told each of us to line up along the wall. She pulled a rubber hose out of her drawer and started spanking each of us one by one until she had finished with everyone. When I went home, my dress and under clothes would not come off. The pain was severe. The sores had dried puss on my clothes. Mother drew up a bath and had me soaking in the bathtub when Daddy got home. His rule was if you were spanked at school, you got another spanking at home. He was furious when he came into the bathroom. However, when he saw the bruises from the hose and the sores that were raw, he went to the phone and called the school. It just so happened, they were not the only parents that had called and complained. The school was quick with their punishment and the teacher was fired. I was so relieved that daddy did not carry through with his punishment that day. The only time I ever remember him not carrying through.

Cia continued to reminisce about her childhood. She wants to understand why things went so terribly wrong. At the same time, she wanted to have had an idyllic childhood. Suddenly she remembered another incident.

Momma was pregnant with her 5th child. She had taken rheumatic fever the month she became pregnant and had been bedfast since the beginning of the pregnancy. She was allowed an hour a day to be up and about. She chose that day to come sit on the front porch and watch us play. Our yard was barren of grass. It was a very sandy lot. She was in her house robe and white fluffy house shoes. When mom looked down at her shoes, they were black. They were covered in sand fleas. Mom saved some and took to the doctor and asked if this is what I could be allergic to. It turned out that was exactly what was biting me and causing all my problems. I had to undergo UV light treatments and more tar medication being put on my sores. After a few months my sores were healed, and the yard had been treated and I was sore free. I was grateful that mom had come to watch us play.

CHAPTER 4

Times with Cousins

Cia was looking forward to her appointment with Sandy Carver this morning. There was something about Monday mornings that Cia always loved. Oh, she knew other folks whined about Mondays, but for her it was always a new start. She gathered her things including her diary. She was a bit anxious as to what would happen during her counseling session.

Kathryn would be coming back to visit today, and Cia was excited to share with her what she had been doing. She was also eager to talk with her about their younger years. Cia hoped Kathryn would have some answers to some of the questions that she had.

Cia sat in the waiting room. The clock on the wall wasn't as loud as it had been the first time. She didn't have to wait long for Sandy. Sandy smiled, and her smile relieved some of Cia's nerves. They walked into her office and Cia took a deep breath. She told Sandy, "I truly love the scent in your candle warmer.

Sandy said, "Thanks. I love it too. "It's called clean linen".

Cia thought it smelled heavenly and wanted to get some for her house.

Sandy asked, "How are the diary entries was going?"

Cia asked, "Would you like to read my diary entries so far?"

Sandy said, "Only if you're comfortable with me reading it."

Cia said, "I was hoping for some critique and whether or not I'm doing it correctly.

Sandy told her, "There is really no right or wrong way to write the entries in your diary. Write the words down as they come to you. The more you write the more of your burden you will put down."

Cia handed the diary to Sandy and waited while she read her entries. When she finished, Sandy handed the diary back to Cia.

Sandy said, "I'm surprised there weren't any happy times in the diary."

Cia told Sandy, "That's why I'm here. I can't remember anything other than sickness and abuse. I haven't even scratched the surface with what I've written so far."

They talked some more about the entries in the diary, how Cia was doing in her current life, and what they might work on in the future. Sandy said, "I'm sorry your childhood was so very difficult. I hope as time goes by you can uncover some happy times."

"Me too," Cia said. "I know it can't have all been bad, but it was bad enough that I still feel a little like I'm raw and bleeding. What's scared over is deep and creates blank spaces in my mind about my life."

When they finished the session and made an appointment for the next session, Cia said, "I want you to know it is marvelous to be heard and not judged. I really appreciate your presence in my life."

"Thank you. Let's keep working on it and I'm sure we can make things better. We can't change the past but maybe we can put a lot of it in the attic."

Cia laughed. "That would be a miracle."

****

Cia drove home and to her surprise Kathryn was waiting on

the porch for her. They hugged and Cia said, "Come on in. Let's sit and talk. I've been wanting to share with you what I've been up to."

Kathryn had not seen the home since all the walls were torn out and the rebuilding starting.

Cia said, "Come let me give you the tour of the house" She shared details about how and what they'd be doing to their new home.

After the tour they went to the trailer. Cia showed Kathryn how the table would fold down and they had gotten an air mattress to go on top for comfort while she was staying there. They sat across from the table in the two recliners. They talked about everything that had been happening in their lives since they 'd been together.

Cia stood up and said, "Now that all the pleasantries are out of the way, I'd like to tell you what I've been doing while the men have been working on our house."

Kathryn smiled and said, "I'm hoping it is all good."

Cia told Kathryn about seeing a counselor.

Kathryn was excited and said, "I'm glad you are getting some help with understanding your feelings and remembering your childhood."

Cia showed her the diary and asked her to read it.

After a bit of tears and laughter, Kathryn looked up and said, "This is a start, but surely that's not all you remember."

Cia told her, "I'm just beginning. So far I've not had a breakthrough with anything that was pleasant in my childhood." Cia continued, "Kathryn I can't even remember grandmother's voice," and she began to cry. When she could speak again, she said, "I remember us being together, but we were always sent outside. I can't remember sitting down with grandmother, I can't remember a hug or nothing. I remember granddad talking to us, I remember sitting in their living room at night and watching he and Aunt Lottie watching wrestling and granddad usually knocked his chair over, fighting with the wrestlers and everyone laughing, but I don't remember grandmother."

Kathryn was very loving and hugged Cia. "It will come, just give it time. You've come a long way already."

Cia pulled herself together and realized she wasn't being a very good hostess. She dried her tears and looked at Kathryn, "Where are my manners? Do you need something to eat or drink or both?"

Kathryn smiled and said, "As a matter of fact I could use a Diet Dr. Pepper." She laughed and knew there would be a stock of them here.

Cia fixed her a drink and they sat and continued to catch up until Cia realized the time was getting late. She noticed Jock was pacing, which meant he was ready for dinner. They decided to go have Mexican and enjoy a relaxing evening.

****

When Cia, Jock and Kathryn arrived home Kathryn said, "I'm exhausted. Ya'll do whatever. I'm going to bed."

They all laughed, hugged and Kathryn went to bed.

Cia said, I'm going to bed and read a bit in my diary to see if anything comes to mind."

Jock followed and when they were in bed, he opened his reading app and read while Cia read in her diary beside him.

She hoped something would come to mind with reading the previous entries. Suddenly a wave of memory flooded her mind. She laughed and started writing.

I recalled an incident when Kathryn and her sister was with me, Martha and our youngest sister. Kathryn and Martha were ahead of the others in school. They were in the first grade and the others were not in school yet. Pretty soon Kathryn and Martha became very upset and afraid. We girls (yes, all 5 of us) were in the station wagon waiting on our moms to do laundry at the laundry mat. They had spotted a sign that read "WHITES ONLY". They both were very upset and getting more upset the more they talked. Kathryn said, "I know that mom took colored clothes in there also. We have to warn them." Martha reminded her that we were told to stay in the car unless one of us were dying. She looked around and said, "No one is dying, but I'm afraid to not go in and tell them." Needless to say, we all started crying and were upset because our moms were going to be in trouble. Finally, mom saw that we were all crying so she came out to see what the problem was. Martha pointed to the sign and stated, "We know you took colored clothes in, and maybe you didn't see the sign." Mom started laughing and said, "You silly girls, that means only White people could come in there." We didn't know what that meant either because we had only been around white people. Mother said, "We will talk more about this tonight at home, but for now don't worry, no laws have been broken." Later at home mother sat us down and explained that not all people in the world had white skin as we did. I don't remember seeing a black person until I was in the 6th grade, but now and again that incident pops into my mind. I thought it rude not to let the black people do their laundry.

Cia closed the diary and thought, that's all for tonight. I'm really tired.

CHAPTER 5

Life in the country

After a wonderful visit with Kathryn, it was time for her to leave. Cia thought, we always have a good time reminiscing and I hate to see her go. We've become as close as close can be without being sisters.

Kathryn and Cia had similar lives as children growing up. Even in adulthood and marriages, they could relate. They could talk with each other about their mothers, their siblings and most of all the way their fathers had treated them and their siblings. Cia was a bit jealous of Kathryn though. Kathryn had a relationship with her grandmother that Cia wanted. Cia and her family had moved away when she was 9 and her grandmother died shortly after she had turned 10.

Cia had not written in her diary while Kathryn was there. There was just not enough time for writing in her diary and catching up or talking about their past. It always helped to talk through things with Kathryn. Cia decided that it was time to try to remember more of her past. She gathered up her diary and writing things and fixed her Diet Dr. Pepper and found a comfy spot on the back porch. It was the perfect temperature so she settled into her favorite chair and began to write.

It was a usual evening at home. While us girls were getting ready for bed, Martha was told there was an envelope under the phone and that we were to take it in the morning as we were walking to school and put in the mailbox. Daddy had started a bakery in Yukon and he and mom would be leaving early and call and wake us up when it was time to get ready for school. Martha was 11 and I was 9 and Elizabeth (Lizzy) 8. We got up and got ready for school. I told Martha, "We have to get our beds made up so we're not in trouble when mom and dad get home." So, we all 3 went into our room and made our beds.

Martha asked, "where's the envelope that we're supposed to take to school with us?" We frantically looked all over the house. We went to every area that we were in that morning. We knew we had to find the envelope, but we also knew that we had to be to school on time and time was running out. We finally decided to go to school and not be late. We knew we hadn't left the house with the envelope so mom would help us find it when we got home. Well, things didn't go exactly like that. The first thing daddy asked was did we take the envelope and put in the mail drop box on our way to school. We said no that we couldn't find it when it got time to go to school, but it must be here in the house because we knew we hadn't taken it out. Daddy became furious, ripped off his belt and started beating on Martha. Mom tried to step in and keep him from hurting her, but he slung mom against the wall and continued beating on Martha. The pictures on the walls were strewn everywhere. Mom was on the floor crying and Martha was screaming in pain and begging daddy to stop. I stood in the doorway crying and wishing I could make it all stop. Finally, the carnage stopped, and mom got up off the floor and took Martha in her arms. They went to the bathroom and mom was trying to help Martha get her clothes off. Her back was bleeding and the wounds looked pretty bad. I was so scared. I was afraid daddy would do the same to Lizzy and myself. I can't even remember having dinner that night. Mom was helping Martha get into bed and when she pulled the covers back, there was the letter. Evidently Martha had laid the letter down when making her bed. I thought surely that there would be an apology or something, but nothing. Martha was hurt so badly that she didn't go to school for the next couple of weeks. I would bring her homework home for her. When the wounds finally healed and she wasn't bleeding, Martha was able to go back to school. She had to take a pillow with her to sit on during the day. I felt so sorry for her and there was nothing I could do to.

****

Shortly after this time Cia's family moved from Bethany. Their father became a pastor of a small church in Southeast Oklahoma at a crossroads called Friendship. Cia fondly remembered this was the first time she felt like a child. She had a close friend Julia Sherman whom she loved dearly. Julia and Cia spent almost every waking hour together. They rode the school bus together, about an hour each way. They would bring a hymnal and sing church songs to and from school. It gave Cia a sense of peace and wellbeing.

I continued to dwell on the year and a half that we were at Friendship. School let out in October each year, when all the kids went to the cotton fields and helped pick the cotton. It was fun because there were lots of kids picking cotton with us. We raced to see who could pick the most. I remember picking about 90 pounds a day. We were paid $.01 per pound. I always laugh. We thought we were making a lot of money, but it was nothing to get rich with.

I taught myself to play piano too. Martha had gotten piano lessons in Bethany, Oklahoma for about six months. I decided to take Martha's old books and learn to play like Martha. Martha helped me with the basics, and I went on from there, just like she did. I loved to sit and listen to Martha play. One day I remembered being in the church practicing when suddenly, I felt like someone was watching me. I looked around and didn't see anyone, but it spooked me just the same. About that time Momma was driving our car into the yard and honking her horn very loudly and often. I decided to go see what all the commotion was all about. By that time, Momma was yelling for everyone to get into the house. We all went inside and locked all the doors and windows as instructed. Then we all went to the living room where mom was and she explained that convicts had escaped from the penitentiary in McAlester, which was 29 miles away. They were believed to be in our area. I told mom about the eerie feeling while playing the piano in the church. The next thing we knew there were several sheriff vehicles in our yard and going down the road in front of the church and our house. The sheriff came to the house and told us that the convicts were down the road from the house and mom told them about me feeling like someone was in the church. They went to the church and went through all the church and came back and told us the church was clear, but that there were footprints in the front area of the church, and they felt like the convicts had been in there. I was really scared. In a few minutes the sheriff came back to the house and let us know that they had appre-hended the convicts in a shed just a 1/4 of a mile from the house and it was all clear for the kids to go back outside and play.

CHAPTER 6

Scary encounters and Broken Bones

Cia continued to think about her time at Friendship. She had been living in Bethany, Oklahoma in a small two-bedroom house. It felt huge to them but was about 1000 square feet total if you were very generous. She chuckled thinking about the house. Cia thought it was a mansion and the yard was huge. When we moved to Friendship the house was nearly as big as the one in Bethany, but we had a much bigger yard and play space.

Cia sighed at the memories of a child and how perspectives changed as she grew older. Regardless, Friendship was mostly fun, but memories of everyday life escaped her. She continued to be concerned her memories weren't any clearer. Then suddenly she remembered a terrifying scene in Friendship. She quickly opened her diary and began to write:

> *There was a man banging on the door. Daddy went to the door and there was a   member of the church standing at the front door and fusing at daddy. Why was he being so rude to daddy? I was scared to move very close because it would upset daddy. I heard the man say to daddy, as he was shaking a saw at his face, "I will see you dead before I see you serve here another year." Then the door closed, and I scurried back to the bedroom before daddy saw me.*
>
> *I heard he and mother talking. Daddy raised his voice and shouted, "I don't know why they are so upset. What do they expect me to do, I just preach what the bible says?"*
>
> *I was really confused and wondered why preaching from the bible would upset people. Mother couldn't explain for us*

why he was upset, and we sure as hell would not ask Daddy to explain.

Later in life I found out why, he was sleeping around and screwing with their wives and other ladies in the community. That's what he didn't want Mom to know or us kids for that matter. In a few Sundays time, the church was full and lots of people I'd never seen. I later found out that people were even from Alaska to vote no for my dad to stay at the church. Mom cried that day and was so upset. I think she had finally had a home that she enjoyed and was proud of. She didn't want to leave, and none of us kids wanted to leave, but we had no choice.

****

The family moved from Friendship to Tecumseh. Cia was amazed at how beautiful the house was that they were moving to. Their house in Friendship was a 2-bedroom house that didn't even have an indoor bathroom until several months after they moved in. This was a 3 bedroom, 2 bath home. Her parents had their room and bathroom and the boys had one bedroom and the girls had a room together. Cia thought they had arrived. After all the siblings had all shared one bedroom in Friendship. Cia wrote about all the episodes in their new home.

I remember having to help with folding all the clothes. Momma said, "you know you moved when everything is washed, folded and put away. I was folding towels with my little sister Lizzy. Lizzy was a bully to say the least. She didn't like the way I was folding the towels and took the broom that was leaning up next to the wall and hit me on the head with it. I passed out. Mom kept calling me to come help her, but I couldn't answer. She came to our room to see what was going on. Lizzy explained to her that I wasn't doing what she wanted so she hit me with the broom. By this time, I was coming to. Mom told Lizzy that she had to finish folding the towels because of how she was treating me. Mom had me come and help her dust and clean furniture. I never minded helping Momma.

Cia chuckled to herself and how Lizzy proved how much of a bully she was. She wrote in her diary:

> *The football player across the street came to meet Martha. Lizzy told him he would have to arm wrestle her before he could talk with Martha. Guess who won? You got it—Lizzy. She was like this with any boys that tried to talk with either Martha or me.*

Cia was beginning to remember a lot of her life. It was in Tecumseh where she began to feel she might be able to be her own person. She wrote about going to school in a bigger school than they'd been going to:

> *I remembered the first day of school at Barnard Elementary school. When Lizzy and I were walking home from school, two boys approached us on bicycles. They were whooping and hollering and trying to get our attention. One of the boys shouted, please stop, I want to kiss you, I've never seen anyone as pretty as you are." Lizzy proceeded to pull the boy off his bicycle and beat on him, his cousin jumped off his bicycle and tried to help but to no avail. She had knocked out permanent teeth and blacked both their eyes and sent them on their way. I went to school in Tecumseh until the 11th grade and those 2 boys would not talk with me. I went back during my senior year and saw the two in the hallway. They asked where Lizzy was, and I told them she was at Texhoma. They came over and talked to me because they knew they wouldn't get beat up.*

Cia continued remembering her childhood in Tecumseh. Her fond memories were coming to light and were a relief to her. She continued writing:

> *Daddy bought a Shetland pony. On the 5th of July in 1966, on a Sunday afternoon Dad brought the pony to the house. There was a field adjacent to our house. The neigh-*

borhood kids all gathered, and we took turns riding the pony. When it came my turn, Daddy had left, and Momma was inside the house watching us girls from her bedroom. I got on the pony which took off running. I hadn't gotten a hold of the reigns and so when the pony jumped the small ditch, I fell off the pony and it stepped on my right arm, breaking both bones. I jumped up and wrapped my arm my shirt. Mom was running out to help her. One of the neighbor boys looked up and said, "I didn't know a fat woman could run that fast". His mother shushed him. Our neighbor across the street took mom and me to the hospital. Martha and Lizzy stayed at the house and kept track of the two younger brothers. There wasn't a phone at the church so that they could let dad know what was going on. When he came back to get everyone to take them to church, he found out what was going on. Our neighbor stayed with us and took us back home once the doctor had arrived at the emergency room and they set my arm. This was a small town, and the family had a bakery on the main street. The doctor would periodically come by and check on me. I could not make a fist or even grip a pencil to write. They did an x-ray, and my bones were not healing. A calcium deposit had formed under the bones instead of between the bones. The doctor decided to take the cast off after 6 weeks and gave me exercises to get the blood to flow better in my arm. The 3rd day after he took the cast off, he asked if I had a jump rope. I said yes and he instructed me to use it several times a day.

I didn't mind, I loved jumping rope. I went out into the back of the bakery. The ground had gravel on it. There was a senior boy at the store next door, taking a break. I had a crush on him big time. His sister and me were friends and I'd make excuses to go to their house so I could see him. Well needless to say, I was trying to show off my jump rope skills. Wouldn't you know, I slipped on the gravel and fell. He sat there just staring at me. I was really irritated. In my mind I thought he would jump and run and help me up. Nope, that didn't happen. Fi-

nally, I was able to get up. I ran into the bakery, which was in a movie studio. The back area was the stage, which was higher than the rest of the building. I jumped off the stage, while holding my arm, and went to where mom was making cookies. I told her that I broke my arm again. Mom called the doctor's office, and they were still there. They told Momma to come on over with me. Mom walked with me to the doctor's office. They gave me a shot for pain. The doctor said it should have put me to sleep but it didn't. They gave me some more medication and it didn't work. The doctor told mom that he couldn't give me anything else and that he would have to reset my arm with me awake. I can tell you that was pretty painful.

When we went home, I slept for 2 days. Mom would wake me occasionally, give me a drink or something to eat, help me to the bathroom, and then back to sleep I'd go. Finally on the 3rd day I was able to stay awake. I went to the bakery with mom and dad that day so mom could watch after me. I felt better, but realized my arm was in a cast again. I remember thinking 6 weeks wasn't enough. Well, evidently not. Mom needed something from the store next door so of course I offered to go. When my crush saw me, he asked what had happened. I told him I'd fallen. All the while I was thinking you know when I fell. He said sorry that he didn't realize I was hurt. Anyway, it was 8 weeks later when I finally got the cast off. My arm was really itchy, and I was thankful to get the cast off. When they took off the cast, I had hair about 4 inches long. I had an uncle who was bald on top. I told him he could grow hair if he'd put a cast on his head for 14 weeks. To the day he died he would still laugh about that. The second time I broke my arm, it healed correctly, and I was able to write prettier than I could before.

CHAPTER 7

Living in a Movie Theater

Cia and her husband Jock were happily busy for a few days celebrating their 11th Anniversary. Cia thought to herself, I can't believe how lucky I am to have found my soul mate so late in life. She felt, life was truly wonderful for herself and Jock. Jock loved being back home in his native Louisiana. Yes, Cia thought, he is surrounded not only by his family heritage but his native Cherokee heritage.

After Cia finished putting away the clothes she'd folded, she straightened up the house a bit. She looked around the living room and smiled. She loved the way the room was both modern and a hundred years old. She sighed and said, "Enough puttering. I want to write!"

She picked up her diary and pen, fixed herself a nice glass of Diet Dr. Pepper and went out to the screened in porch. She sat in her favorite chair and read her previous entry. She realized that in the middle of the broken arm, getting it out of a cast and breaking it again, another big change had happened. The beautiful house they had been living in was on the market to be sold. They had to find a new place to live.

Our parents established a bakery out of the garage and kitchen in our first home in Tecumseh. Now, they had to find a different place for their bakery. They liked having the bakery combined with our home, so they looked for a small building like that. They wanted it big enough for the family and for the bakery and not cost too much. After all, money was tight, and we kids could understand that.

The small church was closed because it could not bring in enough funds to provide for the utilities, much less a pastor and family. Daddy found a small movie theater building. The building had a large stage with a movie screen still hanging there. Momma fixed up the space for her and daddy's bedroom on one side of the back door and a family room which included our upright piano on the other side of the room. Just down from the stage was an area where the dining table and chairs were setup. Then the baking areas with huge dough table, big standing mixer and large pizza ovens were installed.

There was a small patron area in front, where the snacks for the theater were located. There was a small room behind the front area where Daddy put in a sink. The room was where we washed all the dishes. The bathroom and shower were just past the showcase in the front. In the projection room upstairs were two rooms but no closets. All three sisters' beds were set up there. Momma pounded in big nails in the stairwell so we could hang our clothes up. Our room was always blistering hot in the summer. It was miserable! Conversely, in the winter it was winter very toasty.

We girls were awakened every day at 5:30. We would get dressed and come downstairs. No piddling around was allowed. We had donuts to cook and glaze before we would leave for school. Daddy had been up mixing the doughs and getting the grease and glaze ready. When we came downstairs, we would cook off the donuts, glaze them, eat a few, and head out for school.

Daddy had to be through by 6:30 as he'd taken a job to drive a school bus. He would be back shortly after we left for school and would help Momma. He would make cinnamon rolls and bread as well as help Momma with sales up front.

Momma had learned how to decorate cakes when she was bedfast. One of our aunts had brought mom books, frosting and tips so she could learn. She was always very artistic, so it was easy to pick up. The bakery flourished and other than smelling like donuts when we went to school, we really had a decent life at this point.

Cia took a break to walk around the yard. The gardens were really coming along nicely. She could hardly wait until spring when everything was in bloom. As she walked, she continued to remember about starting Junior High School in Tecumseh. She chuckled to herself and said, "Cia, it's time to go back to the porch and write."

I enjoyed feeling older and not having to work all day long. I loved having friends and being able to talk and play with them during our longer lunch period now that we were in junior high school. I was allowed to join the pep squad and felt important and excited. On Friday nights, football games were the best. Daddy would drive the bus with the pep squad to the football games. It was the first time I remembered having good times with Daddy. It felt good.

I was also a member of the choir. It meant I would get to go to different places. I remembered starting my period for the first time. I was getting ready to go to Tri-State, a big weekend when all the schools in Oklahoma and the surrounding states would get together for competition. That morning as I was getting ready for the day, I saw blood on my underwear.

I went to Momma and told her about the blood. She gave me A sanitary pad and told me how to put it in my pants. That's all that was said. Momma knew I would be gone for 3 days, but she did not help prepare me for why I was bleeding. I was confused but thought surely someone will tell me why I'm bleeding. I remember being embarrassed about the whole thing and didn't want to say anything to anyone.

When we arrived at Enid, I found a bathroom and to my surprise the pad was full, soaked with my blood. I took off the pad and got lots of toilet paper and lined my panties with it. I knew I would have to keep a close eye on the bleeding. I looked in bathrooms for a dispenser but there was none. I continued to do this for the next 3 days until we arrived at home. So instead of enjoying my first big outing as a teenager I had to worry that people would know I was on my period.

Momma was upset and asked me, "Why didn't you ask for more pads? I would have given you more." I was stunned that she blamed me. She thought I should have asked for more pads when I didn't even know what was going on. Everything had almost worked out okay. On the way home I could feel the oozing blood. It was dark in the bus, so I touched myself. Well, I shouldn't have because now I had blood on the front of my skirt.

I was so embarrassed. I tried everything I could think of to keep it from being noticed as I was getting off the bus and getting to home to the bakery. The next day I showed my new skirt to Momma. She soaked it in cold water and was able to get the blood stain out. I promised myself then that I would never have a daughter of mine not knowing what to do when her periods started. I'd be sure she understood what was happening and having what they needed.

Cia needed a break. She went to the kitchen, fixed herself some lunch and watched her favorite soap opera. A few minutes into the program she began to cry and for the first time in a long time, was glad no one was with her. She needed the tears and the relief of understanding she wasn't given the care and support a mother should give her children. When she was able to quit crying, she said, "I have to keep going and writing. I need it all out. It feels like a boil needing to be lanced."

From this point forward I really did think I had a reasonably good life. I was able to talk with both Mom and Dad when I felt the need. If I asked and was told no, then no was what it was. I had watched Martha and Lizzy do things that went against what the parents had told them, and they were whipped. Not beaten like in Bethany or Friendship but whipped. Then things started changing during my sophomore year.

Martha, who was a senior at this point, had tried talking to Daddy about wanting to live with her boyfriend in Norman and going to college there instead of at Bethany, where Mom and Dad wanted her to go. He had told her no, but Martha continued to try to get him to understand. I thought to myself 'this is not going to turn out well and Martha needs to just stop and let it rest.'

The next thing I knew, dad had ripped off his belt and was slinging the belt at Martha and continued to chase her around the big room. He was beating on her with the buckle end of the belt. I thought I was screaming this out loud, 'please everyone just stop', but no one was hearing me. I was crying and screaming inside myself. When I looked around, I was curled up to the wall and grabbing for something to hold onto and nothing was there.

The beating finally stopped. Martha stormed upstairs to our room and when I thought it was safe, I went upstairs to check on her. I just couldn't understand how Martha would even ask this of daddy. I also couldn't understand how our father could continually be this way to Martha. It was like he hated her. I know she hated him and quite frankly, for good reason.

By this time Martha was working outside the bakery at the nursing home. When she got to work that day, they helped her with the cuts on her skin. They also notified a teacher who'd taken Martha under his wing and asked if he could step in. You know this was back when children weren't taken into consideration much with child welfare. Things like being beaten and brutalized were brushed under the rug. If things had been more like today, we would have been taken away a long time ago.

The schoolteacher went to my father and told him to leave her alone and then he started working through Martha's emotional needs and how to pick a good mate. He had gotten her a residency during the summer of Martha's Junior year, that is where she met her boyfriend. Now that she was in her senior year, Martha was feeling grown and needing to spread her wings. Daddy didn't understand this.

I vowed to myself that day that I would never cross mom or dad and would not do anything for dad to become this upset with me. It was life or death for me.

Cia thought to herself, I am spent after remembering all of this. I will have to continue another day. She closed her diary and whispered, "Martha I'm glad you lived." She brushed tears away knowing there was much more that needed to be written, said at least on paper, but she needed a break.

CHAPTER 8

Moving to a new Town

Cia was pretty shaken up by her last entry in her diary. Reliving all the abuse and not understanding where it was coming from was difficult for her reconcile. After all, her father preached about kindness, being good, loving your neighbor. He even talked about family prayer time and reading the bible. Cia wondered why this was not part of their family.

They went to church. They went to all their cousins Vacation Bible Schools, and they attended with her. She had asked God to come into her heart. Wasn't he in her parents' hearts? Where was the compassion that they were supposed to be showing?

Cia called Sandy Carver, her therapist. She needed to see her a few days earlier than usual. She wanted to go over all the trauma she'd written about. She wanted to work her way through it all. They set an appointment for the next morning.

When Cia sat down in Sandy's office, she said, "Thank you for working me in. I needed to talk it all out."

"I'm glad you called and felt safe enough in our relationship to ask for help."

Cia's lip trembled. She couldn't speak so handed her diary to Sandy.

Sandy took the diary and started reading. After reading the last entry Cia had written, Sandy looked up to Cia, who was weeping quietly. She said, "Cia, I am so sorry that you had all this dished out on you as a child. Living in fear is not a way any child should be saddled with. "I'm proud of you and all you've accomplished in your life, despite the horrible childhood. You are a good woman, have raised good children, and are kind and giving. You are the example of a good parent. Trust me on this: there are still a lot of bad parents out there. You may not have turned your back on your parents, but you did turn your back on abuse and didn't make it a part of your parenting."

Cia felt relief in her words but knew she had struggled even as an adult with abuse. Up until eleven years ago, her life had been in great turmoil and other men treated her exactly like her father had treated Martha. She had always dreamed of a prince charming who would come and ride in on his white horse and save her from all this. She learned the hard way. Prince Charming was just for fairy tales.

When Cia returned home, she sat looking at her diary in her hands. She wasn't sure she could even open it, much less write in it again. Her life was so much different now than it had ever been. She was happy and safe now. She honestly couldn't believe how she or Martha lived through those frightening years.

On the other hand, Cia felt it was important to get her past down on paper so she could deal with it all. She wanted more than anything, to move forward in her life. She opened her diary and started writing again.

> My sister Lizzy and I were so excited. We were moving to a new town. We would all have a chance to start over in a new school where no one knew them. Her parents had been given a pastorate in the panhandle of Oklahoma. Texhoma was a small town that straddled the states of Oklahoma and Texas. Most everyone knew everyone.

> It was a small church but had lots of teenagers who attended. The trip from Tecumseh to Texhoma was about six hours. The members had brought cattle trailers to move us out there. When we were in Woodward, Oklahoma, about halfway there, Daddy called and told them we would be late getting

there. He asked if they could have the beds setup. We could handle the rest.

Supposedly there wasn't going to be anyone at the house when we got there. Right????? Well, on the way there I curled my hair with Dippty-Do. Do you remember that??

When we arrived, there were several vehicles still at the house. We walked in and it seemed like a hundred or more boys were at our house. Of course, there wasn't, but I thought to myself there were at least five or six. Lizzy and I giggled and ran to our room. I immediately took out the rollers, and of the course the Dippty-Do wasn't dry, so I brushed out as good as I could.

We returned to the living room, to greet all the new boys. Those who knew me in those days, knew I was boy crazy and man I felt like I hit the jackpot. We visited for a bit and finally the boys all left. They promised to look for us girls the next day at school and would show us around.

I felt so good! Finally, something fun to look forward to. The boys were nice and mannerly. I felt like a princess, with everyone clamoring for my attention. I had to re-roll my hair again. This time I didn't use Dippty-Do. I figured there was already enough in my hair.

Then to bed. It was impossible to sleep that night. I was excited and trying to figure out what I would wear the next day to school.

First day of school at Texhoma was wonderful. First, we didn't have to get up at the butt-crack of dawn. We were able to have a nice breakfast and get dressed and be to school on time. We didn't smell of donuts either. Even better, the school was across the street from our house. The boys met us as they had promised, showed us to the principal's office and helped us get enrolled. Then they showed us where our classes were. I was in heaven.

The boys were nice. The girls not so much. It seemed I'd struck a nerve and the girls didn't like it. Boys were paying attention to me and Lizzy and not so much to them. I was finally popular, for what that was worth. I decided this was actually a good move and I would not be upset with my parents.

Things were better at home now. Martha was in college and had not made the move to Texhoma with them. She was majoring in English and Music at Bethany Nazarene College. She wanted to play piano and write. She was awesome at both. I always wanted to be able to play piano like her. I was sure she was probably more at peace than she had been in a long time, without mom and dad right on her heels noticing every move she made. I sure hoped she was.

I was 16 now and could drive a car. I passed the tests and got my license just before we moved to Texhoma. This gave me freedom I had not experienced before. I quickly found a waitressing job and was making money of my own. I enjoyed that. I bought all my own personal things and didn't have to ask for them from mom and dad.

I made decent money and was glad to have the freedom of not being at home in the evenings. I felt as if I had finally arrived at a place where peace could be found. For the most part that was way things were. There was some heart ache, as falling for boys will do, but there were no beatings, no yelling and lots of time to play cards with mom and not have to just work all the time.

I lost about 30 pounds when we first moved there. I decided it was because I wasn't in the bakery all the time cooking and cleaning and eating anything I wanted. I realized my clothes were getting very loose on me. Mom altered my clothes, so they fit me better.

Momma and Daddy opened another bakery. A lady in the church needed work and so she helped them with the bakery. This was a big relief for me and Lizzy. Our two brothers were old enough for school then, so mom even had an easier time.

Cia closed her diary and thought to herself, now that was much better today. She sure wished things would have stayed so easy for them, but of course it was not longed lived. Not even a year long.

CHAPTER 9

Perils of Living in Small Town

Cia reminisced about her days at Texhoma. It helped her to be more settled in her heart and mind. They were mostly very good days. She was well liked and felt like she finally belonged. She made some awesome friends and acquaintances. Cia however remember only one time when things were bad for her and Lizzy.

Martha had come to Texhoma with our aunt, whom she had been living with, and a cousin. It was good to see her, or so we thought. The first night, our cousin and Lizzy and I were playing outside and swinging on the stop sign. Well as our luck would have it, it fell off the post. It scared us to death. We didn't know what to do. Our cousin told us to hide it until in the morning and his mom would know what to do.

The next morning, we needed milk to finish up breakfast. Our aunt took me to the store so I could get a gallon of milk. While waiting in the car, our aunt heard a lady talking about me. She didn't say anything to me until we got back to the house. When we were seated at the table our cousin told his mom what had happened to the stop sign and wanted to know what to do.

She said not to worry that she'd call the city and they would fix it. Then our aunt looked at me and asked if I had noticed the lady coming out of the grocery store as I was going in.

"Yes, she is the town gossip, and a member of our church. Why?"

My aunt told me that she was telling the delivery boy

that I was pregnant, and her son was going to have to marry you to save face.

I was in shock. I was still a virgin. I started to talk with my aunt and Martha butted in and said, "That's all my father needs in a new town is to have a whore and hood." Then she stormed out of the house and started walking to the bakery.

Lizzy and I were scared to death. Martha wasn't very nice to her sisters growing up. We felt like it was because of the way she was treated and just tried to stay out of her way.

We started crying and asking the aunt to take care of us. About 10 minutes later the phone rang and it was daddy and he wanted us to the bakery immediately. Our aunt told us not to worry that she would handle this.

She drove us to the bakery and as we walked into the bakery daddy ripped that belt off. Our aunt got between us and daddy. She told him that he would have to kill her to get to us. This was the first time that anyone had stood up for us. She explained what had happened and daddy backed down from our aunt. Although it might have been easier to have gotten a whipping.

He made Lizzy and I break up with the boys we were dating. It was very hard to do.

Cia stopped writing to ponder why Martha would have done that to them. Jock came to the porch and realized that Cia was crying.

Jock said, "What's wrong Cia?"

Cia said, "I've been writing about Texhoma, when Martha came and told daddy I was a whore. I've been trying to wrap my head around why she thought that of me."

Jock told her, "Just think about what all she had gone through to that point, maybe she thought this would bring her into good graces with your father."

"Wow Jock, I hadn't thought about it in those terms. If I had been treated like Martha had been treated her whole life, I might lash out at people also. I really think this was daddy's responsibility for making Martha feel so unwanted. He never let up on her, even after she was married. After all, daddy could have asked about things. He could have believed his daughter instead believed the town gossip. He could have cared about his daughter's feelings. He did none of that."

Jock brought her close to him and wiped away the tears. "I love you too much to watch you suffer. I hope this gets easier for you."

Cia loved Jock's touch and understanding. She was able to clear her head and continued to write in her diary.

> Cia and Lizzy's punishment continued at least for most of the rest of the time we lived in Texhoma. We were allowed to go to the teen activities. We had a great leader who was 30. It was his mother who was the town gossip. He helped with me being able to see my boyfriend. He would come and pick Lizzy and me up to join the rest of the group. He had a basement in his home with a nice pool table. When it snowed and we couldn't have school, we would spend most of the day and evening at their house and be with everyone. We went to bowling activities, and he would be sure to be the one to take us back home. My boyfriend continued to come to church just so he could see me. I let dad know he wasn't scared of him. Daddy never let up.

> We lived there from January to December of 1969. Just around Thanksgiving time, the town gossip walked into the church. She was pleased as punch with herself that day and grinned at me. Soon her 6-year-old granddaughter bounced into the church. Her dad quickly followed. She blurted out to me, "Are you going to be my new momma?"

I was shocked and told her she must be mistaken.

"Nope she continued, that's what my grandma said".

I looked at our leader and he said he would explain later. When we were in Sunday School, he explained that his mother had told him I was pregnant and to save their family name, that she had a dress picked out and showed him the wedding invitations. You see since he would come and pick us up, she assumed that we had been dating. Which we hadn't. I was hoping to be able to explain to daddy, but of course he knew better.

He went to the phone after church and called the district superintendent and told him he needed to be moved. The DS had him to wait so he could see what he could find. In a few minutes the DS called back and told daddy of a home mission church in Magnolia, Arkansas. Dad accepted the position and that evening, turned in his resignation to the church.

Everyone was shocked including us girls. We were heart broken. We loved being in that school and town.

December 18, 1969, we were moved to Magnolia. The principal of the school begged daddy to leave us until school was out. This was my senior year, and I was the secretary helper for the principal. Daddy refused. After all, the reason he wanted to move was to get me away from the one guy that had ever truly loved me to that point.

The church gossiper couldn't let it rest, after we had moved, she called to the Sunday School Superintendent in Magnolia to ask if I had had my baby. He was a good man and didn't tell daddy but told me directly. I assured him I was still a virgin and told him all that had happened to us. He knew there had been some trouble but didn't know what. He was a caring man and was very kind to us girls.

Cia reflected on the things that happened in Texhoma. She remembered thinking her father would never approve of anyone for her. She sighed and shook her head. She told Jock, "I felt terribly disappointed and was truly pissed because we had to leave the place I fit in the best."

CHAPTER 10

Dreaded Move Again, Leaving Everything

Cia sat thinking about the first day at Magnolia. It was nothing like her first day in Texhoma. No one was there to meet us and welcome us. Cia was upset because she had much different plans for her life, and Magnolia, Arkansas was nothing like her plans. She picked up her diary and started writing:

> *I remember that first afternoon. Mom already had the house decorated for Christmas. Christmas tree and all. I swore that sometimes Momma just twitched her nose, and the house was put together. I was never able to keep up with her.*

> *There was a knock at the door and Cia hurried to open the door. Surely this was some of the church people. The man at the door introduced himself as the District Superintendent and wanted to make sure we had made it and had everything that we needed. He was a nice enough man, but it didn't change the fact that I didn't want to be there.*

> *He sat and talked with us. He specifically asked me if I was glad to be there. I was honest and told him no. I explained how my life had been ruined. He wanted to know what he could do to make things better. I told him I had already applied to go to International Institute through my previous district and now she would be ineligible to go. I explained I felt it was my last chance. It was only offered to Freshmen through Senior years. He told me to not worry, and he would have my application sent to him. He would allow it to go into the mix. He couldn't guarantee me a spot and explained his own daughter had to go through what everyone else did. That helped some*

but it didn't bring back the people I had left behind me and I couldn't tell him much with Momma and Daddy standing around listening to every word.

Cia continued to remember those early days in Magnolia. At least there was a couple of weeks before she had to face school.

First day of school came. I had come from a class of 36 and now there was 306 in her Senior class. Shock was not a strong enough word. The campus was bigger than any college that she had seen to date.

Lizzy and I went to the office first. We were told there was an assembly first and we should make our way there. No one told us where this was. There were two white girls walking by us. I said, "Excuse me," and before I could say another word the girls screamed and ran.

Then there was a black girl that came by, this was the first time I had been around very many blacks. There was one in Tecumseh in the whole high school and none in Texhoma. The black girl asked how she could help us and even walked us to the auditorium.

We became great friends.

It was cold and the lockers would not open. I was late several times to classes. Finally, I went to the principal and explained the problem. He helped me get my locker unstuck and walked me to English class and explained to the teacher.

She was a real bitch and absolutely hated me. She always treated me like dirt. I tried to do things like the teacher wanted but she always gave me a bad grade. I had friended a girl that sat next to me and asked for help. The friend looked at my paper that had a big F on it. My friend told me the paper was a good paper and did not warrant that grade. They agreed to switch papers the next day just to see what happened. When they got their papers back, the friend had an A, and I had an F.

> *They took their papers to the principal and explained what they had done. He called the teacher in and confronted her. He then changed both students to another teacher and the first teacher had her contract revoked.*
>
> *I couldn't believe it. Someone had stood up for me again. The rest of the term went without incident.*
>
> *The only problem was I missing my friends in Texhoma.*

Cia stood up and walked around the house a bit. She was so happy where she lived now and loved her home. It didn't make up for everything in her life, but it helped a lot. She refilled her glass and went back to her diary. She had more she needed to write.

> *I was at home doing homework when the phone rang. I answered and it was her boyfriend from Texhoma. He asked if there was a problem because he'd been writing to her and had not had an answer.*
>
> *Back in the 70's there weren't cellphones. It cost to call long distance. I told him that I'd never received any letters. He doubled checked her address, and then I turned to my mom and asked if they had received letters from him. She told her 'Yes, but your dad made me tear them up and throw them away.'*
>
> *He begged for me to let him come get me and get me out of the controlling situation. I wasn't 18 yet and knew Daddy could keep me from going. I begged him for more time, but he wasn't willing to wait. I hung up the phone and felt sure my life was officially over.*

****

Cia paced back and forth across the room remembering how lost she'd felt in those moments. She'd kept her head down and worked as much as she could to stay out of the house and away from her parents. She made good money at waitressing and totally enjoyed the job and the people. It was nothing for her to have $100 at the end of the night.

She chuckled to herself about the money that seemed to be so much back then. Still, it was money she'd made from her own hard work. She never let her dad know how much money she was making. He would have wanted it and it wasn't his.

During her freshmen year in college, she moved out because her dad had started being unbearable to her and demanding to know exactly where she was and why. She was able to get into one of the dorms. Her mom worked at the cafeteria there so she could see her mom every day.

Her mother finally convinced her to come back home, and she was never bothered by her dad again. But she remembered the feeling of how tenuous her life had been at that time. It was just like walking on eggshells and not a very pleasant way to feel.

Cia picked up her diary and pen, then went to sit on the back porch and write.

> There was a new boy in her life, Jamie Toimin. He came to church one day. He looked scruffy, but I wanted him to feel welcome. Jamie latched onto me though. He was a smooth talker. I later found out he was the baby of 14 kids and his parents were very poor. I was only allowed to date guys in the church and Daddy thought it was funny when 3 boys would show up and want my attention. I finally went out with Jamie. You guessed it: I lost my virginity that night. When later I realized I was pregnant I knew life would never be the same.

> I couldn't tell my parents. I told him and begged him to marry me. He told me he would oblige because after all he had the queen of the church, as he called me. It was a quick wedding and daddy couldn't stop me because I was 19.

I had just jumped from the frying pan into the fire. Later I found out he had criminal a record a mile long and it was as nasty as he looked. He ran around on me, including the night we married.

My parents were moving from Magnolia to North-west Oklahoma to Freedom, near Mooreland, OK. Jamie and I moved with them. I was pregnant with my first child and really wanted to be close to my parents.

After their first child, Terrance Wayne, was born he continued to be with other women and failed to take care of me and our son.

I gave up, left my husband, and moved back to my parents' home. They were willing to help and didn't give me a lot of hassle. Within a couple of weeks, a Chaplin called and said my husband was threatening suicide if I didn't go back to him. Daddy insisted I return to my husband. I reluctantly went back to him, after all I had promised to love honor and cherish until death do us part.

Things were not any better. If anything, they were worse. He took me to his parents outside of Magnolia. I was pregnant again with our second child. He refused to let me get medical care and said his mother could deliver her baby. When I was 7 months pregnant, I was ill and so was my 9-month-old baby, Terrance Wayne Toimin.

One of my friends called Mom and told her that it wasn't that I was homesick, but I was sick. She told Momma about me being pregnant again and how frail I was now. A deputy in the Sheriff's office was in the church there and dad called and asked for a welfare check. He reported back to dad about how frail and sick I was.

My parents came from Freedom, OK to Norman and picked up Martha. They drove to Magnolia to rescue me and my baby. When they got there as they were walking out of our house and loading me and Terrance in the car, Jamie followed with a shot gun, and his arm around a woman. He pointed the gun at us. About that time, about 10 sheriff officers stood out of the bushes and made him put the gun down. He was laughing with his arm around his latest conquest.

I weighed only 111 pounds and was 7 months pregnant. When my parents got me to the doctor, they found out I had toxemia poisoning and Terrance was very malnourished. They told my parents I would have been dead if they'd of waited another week. My parents nursed me back to health and helped me until I had delivered my second son, Matthew Glen Toimin.

Cia wept over how close she and her first two children had come to dying. She knew she'd made a mistake but gave thanks her family was strong enough and caring enough to help her when her life was at stake. She knew her life had many more ups and downs she would write about. She thought to herself, well at least mom and dad tried to help me, or did they?

CHAPTER 11

Ending of First Marriage

The next day as Cia was contemplating all the things that had happened to her during her brief one-year marriage. She told Jock, "I've always wondering what it was I did wrong."

He shook his head and said, "My guess is the only thing you did wrong was in the choice of husband. At that time in your life, you were desperate to get out from under your father's hand. Then you were also at a point sexually where you really needed the experience but didn't understand about birth control. You were left with few options."

She nodded. "I appreciate your words and they help some of the pain but still I was the one who had sex with Jamie and pushed hard to be married to him."

"Did you love him?"

"I don't have any idea. Back then, love wasn't something I really understood. I think I probably need to keep writing in my diary and talk about it with Sandy."

"I agree but I hope you'll let go of at least some of the guilt. You were trapped and didn't understand you were jumping from the frying pan into the fire."

She laughed. "That's exactly how it felt. Thanks for talking with me. I think I'll get busy writing in my diary, and you need to get busy on all those rocks in the garden."

He grinned. "I'd hoped you'd forgotten about the rock border."

"Not a chance!"

My first husband, Jamie Toimin, was nothing but a low life in the minds of everyone around me. I soon learned they were right, and I'd made a terrible mistake. I suffered greatly while married to him. I'd expected him to care about me and our baby I was carrying. Those expectations were quickly dashed.

After Momma, Daddy and Martha came and took me home, I was feeling better. A few weeks of being in my parents' care, the parsonage phone rang. Daddy answered, "Nazarene Parsonage".

The voice on the other end stammered and stuttered and said, "Well there must be some mistake."

Daddy asked who he was and who he was looking for.

The voice said, "I'm in Sheriff in DeKalb, Texas. I have a young man here, Jamie Toimin, who says he is your son-in-law."

After being told his name, daddy said, "Yes, he's my son-in-law."

The sheriff said, "I'm confused."

Daddy asked, "Why are you calling about Jaime."

"Well, sir," he stated, "He stole a gun and a car in Magnolia, Arkansas. He crossed state lines and we've caught him and brought him into the jail here in DeKalb."

"Well, I'd say that's a fine place for him to be."

The sheriff continued, "I'm calling to see if you would like to post bail and come get him?"

Daddy chuckled and said, "No you can keep him."

The courts sent him to California and enlisted him into the service for his punishment—that was consider a fine idea in those days. They hoped to make a man out of him.

It did help me, because I received child support for my children. I was able to go to school and work on my degree in accounting and business administration. At least for a short period of time. My education lasted only about a year and a half.

Suddenly the child support stopped, and a call was made to Jaime's CO to see if we could figure out why the child support stopped. Jamie had been given a dishonorable discharge for stealing from the Army during peace times.

Cia wrapped up writing for a bit remembering how demoralized she'd felt. Jaime was a jerk and would never become a good man. She decided to call Sandy and get in to see her again. Cia was glad she had an immediate opening and that she would be able to discuss her feeling about all that had happened to this stage. She felt glad that Sandy wanted to take it slow and discuss things that happened as Cia was writing about them. It helped Cia to put them into perspective.

After a long discussion about what all had transpired during her marriage, Sandy affirmed that Cia had done nothing wrong to cause the marriage to fail. After all, she wasn't the one who had sex with someone else and left her at home their first night. She also wasn't the one running around with anyone that would have sex with him and lie about working overtime. Cia couldn't believe she had been so blind and so willing to do anything, including getting pregnant by someone she barely knew, much less loved.

She said, "I understand now, I had no clue what love actually was. I made my life much worse marrying him than it would have been if I'd just had my baby and make a path for myself."

Sandy nodded. "I understand and in a perfect world that would have been the better choice. Sadly, you didn't live in a perfect world."

Sandy told Cia, "I hope the next part of your life was better."

Cia shook her head. "No, it wasn't, but I really want to write the next part out in my diary before we talk about it all."

"I understand, and it seems to be working for you to write out and then us talk about it each step along the way."

"Thanks, so much for understanding. It really helps a lot knowing I can call, and you'll be ready to talk with me at the first possible time on your schedule. It's a really blessing."

****

Cia went home from her session, feeling some better about her first marriage. She knew nothing would change the marriage but working through it all helped her to understand herself and her choices. She knew she never could have made it work with someone who didn't want her and wasn't interested in having an honorable life. She also knew, wishing that she could have learned this much earlier in life instead of what happened next, was just that—wasted wishes.

She smiled as she pulled up in the driveway of her new home. She told herself, "I'm not going to worry about wishes that didn't come true. Instead, I'm going to work through the rubble and learn how to be the woman I want to be."

Jock waved from the front porch, and she felt a thrill knowing he was a good and honorable man who wanted only the best for her. She'd get there and Jock would help.

After she settled down and Jock was busy again in the yard, Cia sat on the back porch with her Diet Dr. Pepper, diary, and pen. She started writing, ready to get through the next part of her life.

My high school boyfriend from Texhoma called. Mom and dad had seen his aunt and uncle at the doctor's office and found out that I was back home with 2 children and divorced. He called me as soon as he found out. I answered the phone and when Daddy realized who I was talking to, he took the phone away from me and proceeded to tell him he was not welcomed in our family. Daddy told him if he chose to come, he would beat him until no one would recognize him.

I was shattered.
You see, dad was mean to anyone who wanted to date any of his girls. So, my former boyfriend heeded the warnings and stayed away. I was very upset. It felt like a light was finally showing a way forward for my life, but Daddy blacked out the light as quickly as it had come.

I cried for days and tried to make sense of it. I didn't dare go against Daddy. I still remembered how Martha had been treated but I didn't understand how Martha had been able to defy Daddy and marry for love.

Besides, now I had two children. I knew I needed help in taking care of my children. I tried to convince myself that it was for the best. I went to school and to work and tried to make a life for me and my boys. Daddy said I was a sullied woman and no one my age would want me and my boys. I knew that wasn't right because my boyfriend had called, but I didn't dare say that out loud. After all I didn't have enough income to take care of my children and myself.

****

Cia sat and contemplated and wished she'd enough courage and strength to tell her father what she thought of him, but she did not. She'd been scared so much during her early life that she did not feel she could go against her mom and dad. What a pity, she thought. Why didn't I have courage enough to stand up for myself or ask for help from someone else?

One day I had had a severe allergic reaction to something, and Daddy took me to Mooreland, 25 miles away, to the doctor. I was given a shot and sent back home. On the drive back as we went through downtown Mooreland, her dad pointed to the law office of the lawyer, Edgar Tobias, who had helped with getting my divorce from Jamie.

He started talking again about how no one my age would want me. I was Used Material, as he continued to call me.

He said, "You need someone older and more established, that has money to provide for you and your boys."

Later I realized that Daddy was wanting the money he thought a lawyer would have. He hadn't wanted a good life for me and my children. He wanted money for himself. Little did I know that the plans were already in the works for the lawyer to court me.

I thought it was weird, because he was 24 years older than me and what would an older man want with me. In a few days, suddenly, Edgar was there at my parents' house. When I arrived home from school, there he was. His excuse was he had court in Alva that morning and just thought he would stop by and see how things were going and making sure that the child support was still going.

I thought it weird, but I decided to be pleasant, as I'd been taught to be. Similar visits happened over the next few weeks.

Our family were big OU fans. Edgar invited me to an OU football game. He picked me up the next morning and brought me back late that night when the game was over.

I was very excited to go to the game, but unsure

about what was really going on. This pattern of visiting and going to games continued. Edgar was even invited to my parents' home for Thanksgiving dinner. Very soon it was nearing Christmas time. Lizzy was getting married, and of course Edgar had been invited to the wedding. I thought everyone already had us married, but I still had big questions as to what was going on.

The night of Lizzy's wedding was my first time to be invited over to his house. There was a family get-together on Edgar's side of the family, and he wanted me to go. I was hesitant but Daddy was eager for me to go. I was surprised and didn't understand why my parents encouraged me to go to his home overnight. I don't know what is going on.

Well, needless to say, once I was at his house, I quickly figured out what all this meant. Edgar wanted to have sex with me. I felt like I was trapped and had to go along. I was very scared.

Christmas was the next week and when he arrived at my parents' house on Christmas morning, my two children had every toy that a 1- and 2-year-old child could want. The living room floor was full of toys. Then next Edgar brought in a clothes rack with at least 10 different outfits.

Mom had made most of my clothes, so I had had very few clothes from stores. The clothes were on a rolling rack, Edgar had it covered in wrapping paper, when he removed the paper, I could see these weren't from just any store. They were from a fine department store. Momma, Daddy and Edgar insisted I try them on and model them.

Honestly, I felt like I was in heaven. I loved clothes. I couldn't believe how the day had gone and quite frankly didn't understand I was being swept off my feet. It felt amazing and I was happy with all the clothes for me and all the toys for my sweet boys.

Cia contemplated about what she had just written and was wondering how involved her parents were in all this. She said, "Looking back I wish I'd asked why they were doing this."

Jock walked in and asked what was up. She handed him her diary and he read the words. He shook his head and said, "I bet when you figured out what was going on you were confused as to why your parents would do such a thing."

"Yes, I was, and I'll tell you what: Right now, I feel like I was used. My guess is all Daddy cared about was getting money for himself."

CHAPTER 12

Second Marriage

Cia and Jock celebrated their 11th Anniversary. She was happier than she'd ever been in her life. She told Jock, "I can honestly not remember when she felt so happy."

He smiled and said, "I'm glad."

They talked and walked, holding hands. Little things made them both laugh. They truly loved being together. They worked well together, and most of all there were no beatings, no yelling or screaming and very little arguing.

Usually, arguments happened when Cia felt threatened. Jock had learned how to work through those times with her. Instead of getting upset when she didn't understand what he was talking about, Jock had a way of explaining it until she was able to accept and understand his position.

Cia always thought she should have been born in Missouri, because she required being shown what Jock was talking about instead of just taking his word for it. They'd laughed when Cia said, "I know I'm sometimes as stubborn as a mule, but if you just show me, I usually come around."

Jock was happy to oblige and helped her through her issues.

Remembering their wonderful evening celebrating their marriage and how kind Jock was, Cia's mind quickly went to thinking about her diary and what she needed to write next about her previous life.

A few days after Christmas I started running fever

was very sick. I thought I had the flu. After about a week of being sick, Edgar was worried. He called the doctor and setup an appointment for me to see the doctor in Shattuck that afternoon.

I had started my next semester of school. Edgar was there to meet me when I got home. I was in a carpool with 3 other women. This was January 14, 1974. I remembered clearly because it was her my oldest son, Terrance's second birthday. After blood tests were run the doctor came in to visit with me. He first told me that my appendix was about to rupture and would have to come out. I begged to go home for my son's birthday, and he politely told me that my son would like to have me at all his birthdays and not just this one. He was afraid my appendix would rupture before they could get it out.

He also told me I was pregnant again. He told me Edgar wanted him to abort the baby while he was doing surgery. He said he could do that, and no one would be the wiser, but it was up to me.

I couldn't imagine aborting a baby. They were so precious. I didn't even want to talk with Edgar about it. The doctor told me that was fine, and he would take good care of me. Little did I know that the doctor already knew what kind of a man Edgar was. It would have been nice to have been warned.

I missed the first week of college while I was recuperating from surgery. It took a while to catch up, but before long I was in stride with the rest of my class. A week or so later after my surgery Edgar was back at the house and asking Daddy for my hand in marriage. Momma objected, but Daddy sent her to their bedroom and said, 'I will handle this.' He gave his blessings. By the later part of February, we were married.

Cia thought about her mom objecting, why didn't I go talk with mom, why didn't I value myself more than this? She brushed away tears, took a deep breath and continued writing.

Edgar purchased a lot in Mooreland and a 16'x80' mobile home for our home. It was a nice enough home and was already furnished. I was pleased there was a room close to us for my two children, Terrance, and Matthew, to have their room.

I had a set of bunk beds that made into trundle beds to help conserve space in their bedroom. The boys seem to adjust well. They were young and only knew my dad and Edgar as men in their lives. The lot was across the street from the city park which made it easy for me and the babysitters. I liked having a safe place to let the kids run off some of their energy.

One night after the kids were in bed suddenly Edgar became very angry. I could not even remember what I had done to make him angry. Edgar started hitting me. He was very angry I was pregnant and would not let the doctor abort the baby. He was yelling and screaming and flailing about. He started using my abdomen as a punching bag. I was so afraid that he would hurt the baby. I begged him to stop.

Thankfully the baby was not injured, and I delivered him successfully. Slade Jay Tobias was born September 18, 1974. He was a healthy seven-pound baby. Edgar was over the moon with him, but honestly, I was not very happy. I worried about the kind of life that Slade would have. When he was about two weeks old, his older brother Terrance, decided to eat some night shade berries. They are very poisonous, and he had to have his stomach pumped. Edgar wanted me to spend the night at the hospital and he would take care of the baby. The next morning, I called to check on Slade and how he had made it through the night. I wasn't worried about Edgar not feeding him because he had gotten that ritual down. She also knew he had two sisters about ten miles away if he needed help.

Edgar began to tell me about how the night had gone. He was very upset that he had gone through all of Slade's sleepers. There were around ten. He said when he changed his sleeper, he would immediately pee right through them.

I asked if he changed his diaper each time. Edgar's response was he didn't know how. I begged him to bring Slade to me. When he got there with Slade, the doctor was in the room with me. I had told him the story before he got there.

The doctor was appalled that Edgar had not even tried to change the diaper and proceeded chewing at him. He made Edgar take off the urine-soaked diaper. Slade's butt was raw and looked like fresh hamburger meat. The doctor instructed the nurse to get some cream. He showed Edgar how to bath the baby and get as much of the urine off as possible. Then had Edgar to spread the cream over Slade's bottom.

The doctor then showed Edgar how to put on a baby's diaper. He proceeded to take it off and then made Edgar put it on again. The doctor proceeded to tell him that Slade was as much his responsibility as he was mine. He stated after all there are two other young children that I also had to take care of, plus I was trying to recuperate from having a baby.

From that point on Edgar helped with taking care of Slade. Slade had a problem with keeping his formula down. The doctor changed it several times. Nothing seemed to help, so they put him on some medication to be given thirty minutes before any formula. This helped greatly with the projectile vomiting. Slade began to gain weight and was a much happier baby.

After a couple of months, we went to Edgar's mother at her home in Shattuck for Sunday dinner. Edgar's sister was there also. Edgar's mother was holding Slade and trying to feed him some mashed potatoes. First, he wasn't old enough to have that and second, he hadn't had his medicine. Slade was screaming bloody murder and was very upset.

I begged Edgar to pick him up from his mother and he

refused. When I got up from the dining room table to get Slade, his sister hit me and told me to leave him alone, Edgar's mother hit me with her cane and then Edgar started hitting and beating on me.

Terrance and Matthew had already been fed and they were taking a nap, thank heavens. Things finally heated up so badly that I ran out of the house and was headed towards the police station. Edgar chased me down and pulled me back into the house. I'd had all I could take that day and took a hand full of pills trying to end the abuse.

Edgar got scared and called Martha and told Martha that I was out of control and had taken a bunch of pills.

Martha talked with me, and I explained what all had happened. Martha felt so bad for me, but she was in Nebraska at the time and could not come and help me immediately. She talked with me and kept me from going to sleep until I threw up. Once I threw up Martha knew I would be okay, so she let me off the phone. I went to sleep.

Cia shook her head trying to get the images out of her head about the incident. She sighed and said, "I was in way over my head and didn't know how to get out." Cia remember many days not unlike that day. They happened way too often. Cia remembered feeling trapped and in reality she knew she was trapped at the time. Back then, she worked in Edgar's office along with another lady. Cia remembered she always hated to go home because anything and everything would set Edgar off.

CHAPTER 13

Fleeing the Nest for new work

Cia continued thinking about her life and wondering how she was ever strong enough to have gone through all she had gone through. Looking back, it was hard to imagine how anyone could have survived her experiences. She knew it was her relationship with God and her church family who accepted her and helped her. She picked up her diary and began writing about her parents moving to Blackwell, Oklahoma.

We visited my parents in Blackwell for the weekend. I woke up on Sunday morning throwing up uncontrollably. Momma was in the kitchen sautéing onions for her roast that morning. She gave me some crackers and Sprite to try to help settle my stomach. Nothing seemed to help. After lunch, Edgar told my parents he thought he needed to get me and the kids back home. He said, "If Cia continues to be so sick, she'll need help from a doctor."

We gathered things up and left for home. Just being out of the house and not smelling the onions helped a lot. I didn't throw up again. The next day I went to the doctor and the doctor did some tests. He came into the room and was laughing. I asked what was so funny. He said, "You don't have a virus, you have another baby."

I thought to myself, yay, I've got another baby on the way and then I sobered and wondered how Edgar would re- spond to this news. Will he be angry, will I get beaten again? I couldn't tell the doctor all these thoughts. This was my fourth pregnancy in four years. I felt very drained and very tired.

Things progressed well with the pregnancy and for the first time in a long time, I was being treated well. Maybe this would be the time that I would finally be loved.

Edgar had a nephew in Woodward that had 2 younger children, and they became very close. They would come and play games together and the kids could all play together.

I thought, finally a happy family. After August Mikel Tobias was born, I was distraught. I had my heart set on having a girl. When I began to come to after having him, I was being told, you must quit crying, or we'll never get your blood pressure down.

The day August was born I had been working all day at the law office. For lunch we went to the local cafe. Edgar was supposed to have court that day and was granted a continuance due to me being overdue already. The judge happened to be in the cafe also. He could see how miserable I was. I only had a piece of lemon pie. I wasn't feeling well. After lunch we went back to the office so I could finish typing the document I had been working on. It was for the Oklahoma Supreme Court. It was a document in a court appointed case. Edgar took me with him to the post office to mail the document.

While there, the hospital administrator came out. He talked a bit with me and told Edgar, you need to get her to the doctor, she doesn't look like she's feeling well. Edgar took me to the hospital/doctor office combination. He let me out of the car and drove off. He had something he needed to take care of. I waddled into the office. By this time, it was just after three in the afternoon. The shifts were changing at the hospital.

One of the RN's saw me waiting. She came over to me and took my blood pressure. She looked at the lady sitting beside me and said, "Don't panic but if anything happens, scream."

Almost immediately they were taking me back to the doctor's office. My blood pressure was 160/140 at this point. The doctor came in and told me he couldn't let me wait any longer. He explained my health was in jeopardy. They sat me down in a wheelchair to take me upstairs so they could get me ready to have my baby. The pains started and were a minute long and two minutes apart.

I had to stop by the front desk and sign some papers. Edgar was still nowhere to be found. They wheeled me upstairs and rushed getting me setup to have my baby. The doctor was going to break my water, but it suddenly broke and splattered the doctor in the face. I thought it was funny because this doctor had been so awful to me during all of my pregnancies. That's about all that I remembered until hearing, "If you don't quit crying, we'll never get your blood pressure down."

My little boy was perfect. However, I had so wished for a little girl. In fact, I had given away most of the baby clothes I had for my other children and bought little girls outfits.

Edgar had to go buy a little boy outfit to take my baby home in because I had packed a little girl's outfit.

****

Cia reminisced about bringing home her fourth child. She loved her children, but it was a really hard time for her. Her parents had the other three children while Cia was in the hospital. Cia decided to write about this experience.

Edgar brought me to our house in Woodward. We had moved to Woodward due to me expecting a fourth child. The mobile home was just not big enough. Edgar soon left to go to his office. Within a few minutes my parents were there with the other children. I expected mom and dad to stay and help her for a bit. After all, there were four children ages four and under.

They did not stay, in fact, they didn't even want to hold their newest grand baby.

For several hours I was alone with all four children. I thought I'd go crazy with all the noise. The other boys couldn't help it, but the noise was almost more than I could emotionally take. We lived across the street from one of Edgar's sisters. When she got home from work, she came over to be with the new baby.

She was very upset because I was there by herself. She immediately dug in and started helping the older boys get settled down for a nap and helped me with August. She insisted that I go to bed and rest. I did not argue as I was very tired. It had only been three days since I'd given birth.

I quickly went to sleep once in bed. I woke up after what seemed like a minute but was 3 hours later. I smelled something wonderful. My sister-in-law had made supper for the family. She was feeding the younger boys along with Edgar. August was sound asleep. I loved that I could be with all the family and eat in peace.

I just couldn't thank my sister-in-law enough. She told me she would come back every day when she got through with work and for me to not overdo until she could get there every day. She was a life saver, and we became close. She was nothing like Edgar's other sister and his mother. She was loving and kind. I wished she had been around a lot more.

After about two weeks I went back to the office to work. After all I was just sitting and typing. We set up the office for me to have the baby with me. Edgar loved it when August was old enough to take to the drugstore for ice cream. He was very active in August's care. At least at first.

Then suddenly Edgar was back to his old self. I didn't know what to do. We argued all the time and usually ended in me being physically assaulted. I decided it would be best if I went to work outside of the attorney office. I talked with Edgar about it, and he agreed.

He said he preferred just having the one secretary. I had talked with an accountant several weeks back about a mutual client. I decided to try to venture out on my own. I was very shy and lacked a lot of self-confidence. I had made a new outfit. The outfit gave me a lot of courage. I'd thought if I could complete a new outfit, surely, I could get a job. I went first to the accountant's office. It was October of 1976. It was the off season for accounting and tax services. I introduced myself as the person who had talked with him previously about our mutual client. He remembered and wanted to know how he could help.

I told him that I was looking for a job and thought that he might need some help. He responded by saying, 'I do. I wasn't planning on hiring until after the first of the year, but I could make an exception for the right person.' I continued to let him know that I'd been doing income tax work for three years now and that I had two years of college for accounting and business administration behind me. I let him know I'd hoped to continue my education as soon as I could.

He hired me on the spot. I was to report to work the next day.

When I arrived back at the office, Edgar in his snarky voice, said, 'Well how did your job hunting go?'

I responded, "Great. I got a job and will start tomorrow."

Edgar was stunned. He thought I would be turned down and not be able to find work. After all, he thought I was stupid and couldn't do anything right. It didn't matter that I had turned his office around and that he was finally making money for the first time since he opened his office in 1955.

August was now four months old, and he would be able to go to daycare with the other kids. Edgar wouldn't have to have the children in the office, and I would get a break from the abuse and the children. Win, win in my book.

CHAPTER 14

Perils of Working and Losing a Child

Cia loved working for the accounting firm. It was her first real job other than waitressing. During her time there, she felt she grew a lot as an individual and was proud of her progress. Cia felt her life was finally evolving from being controlled by others, then she thought, "*well, not so much. Both Daddy and Edgar want to control everything I do in life.*"

She dressed for the day and then told Jock, "I want to write some more in my diary."

"Sounds good to me. I'm going down to the lumber yard and see if I can find some scrap wood for projects in my work room."

She laughed. "And have some man-time with the fellas too."

He shrugged his shoulders. "Well, somebody has to do it."

She smiled as he walked away. She knew her life had blossomed when she met Jock. She was eager to get back to writing in her diary and see if she could banish a few ghosts.

My first day at the accounting firm, I was so excited I went to work early. Some of the other people there showed me to my office. My office—my very own space--was at the front of the office. I was pleased I'd be part of the action. My desk was positioned across a window. I would be helping people as they brought in their information. The boss told me my job was the most important in the office. I needed to help people feel at ease and help them any way I could. As the day progressed, my boss brought more and more things for me to do. I was able to accomplish them with ease. I loved working with numbers.

The second day he told me how pleased he was with my work and wondered if I wanted to learn more. I was excited and of course accepted the challenge. He showed me a spreadsheet that they did for a lot of their clients. I'd loved doing spreadsheets in college, and felt I was finally going to use some of my education. I completed the first one with ease. My boss said, 'I just knew you'd be a great addition to our office and you're not disappointing.'

I felt very proud of myself and thought 'screw you Edgar for thinking I couldn't do this.' I loved my job.

****

Cia made another appointment with Sandy to discuss what she had written since her last visit. Sandy was very accommodating and had an opening that day. Sandy read over her diary since the last visit.

She said, "Cia I'm so sorry you had to go through so much trauma. I especially hate it increased your burden of taking care of so many children. It could have been a time of joy and love."

Cia nodded. "I never felt the kids were the burden. Actually, they were my lifeline." She sighed. "The real burden was Edgar. If he'd really loved me, he would have been helping me and finding ways to make my life easier.

Sandy shook her head. "You're right. He was supposed to be your helpmate in life. Do you have any idea why he beat you so often?"

"I think thought Edgar beat me because he was so upset about his own life. His mother was very controlling. He'd never been able to get away from her. Being the baby of the family meant everyone was vying for his attention."

"Has he verbalized those feelings to you?"

"No, but I remember his mother telling me I was taking her son away from her. She told me she would never like me for that reason alone. I still didn't pity Edgar though. He was mean and abusive not only to me but to my oldest son, Terrance."

They talked a bit more and then Sandy said, "I like how you are facing the demons in your life. Keep on writing and letting yourself feel what should have been as well as what happened. Keep your heart open for yourself."

****

Cia drove home, thinking about all Sandy and she had talked about. She glanced in the rear-view mirror and smiled. She said, "Girl it's high time you figured out how to handle your grief and anxiety over your life before you met Jock." She chuckled and thought, *I'll keep writing and learning more about myself.* When she got home, she went to the back porch with her Diet Dr. Pepper, diary, and pen. It was time to write some more of her life.

I remember that Matthew and Terrance were sickly children. The doctor started giving them IGG shots to help boost their immune systems. Terrance rallied but Matthew did not. By June of 1977 the doctors told us Matthew needed to have his tonsils taken out. I remembered having mine out and since they said that Matthew was failing to thrive and could possibly die from an infection, I agreed to let them do the surgery. Momma came to be with me so that she could take care of Matthew during the day while I continued to work. Two weeks after the surgery Matthew was still unable to eat. We had to let his cereal soak and become mush and then he could eat a bite or two.

I remember this day as if it had just happened. We were watching the Walton's on TV. Daddy was there so he could take mom back home. I thought it was safe since it had been two weeks since his surgery. However, that evening, he choked and started coughing. Suddenly, it was like a water hose in his mouth spewing out blood. Immediately there was a large puddle of blood.

Momma scooped Matthew up in her dress tail and ran to their car. Daddy was running ahead of her and opening doors. I quickly followed close behind them. The hospital was just two blocks away. When we got there Edgar had called ahead and we were rushing to get Matthew into the emergency room. Matthew had bled so much he didn't have enough blood to cross match so they could give him more blood.

When the young doctor arrived, the hospital administrator had gotten there about the same time. The doctor jumped from his car and ran to the emergency room. He didn't even put his car in gear. The administrator jumped into his car and parked it and put it in gear. The young doctor told the nursing staff that the child had been born there and to get his records.

He said, 'We know there were no incidents during his birth so we need to lay his mother down and take blood from her and give to him, we can replace mom's blood.'

About that time the older doctor walked in an told everyone that they weren't approved to do that at this hospital. So, they gave Matthew plasma and vitamin K. Matthew rallied and became stable. They took him upstairs and admitted him. The next morning, they gave Matthew a blood transfusion, but he started bleeding again. They were able to get the bleeding to stop after a little while.

They let Matthew try to eat, which they brought red gelatin, and Matthew cried because it looked like blood. Momma asked if they had any other color and they said, yes, we should have thought of that.

Matthew continued to rally and get better. The young doctor came in and talked with me and mom and explained that he wasn't for sure what was going on, but he knew things were not right. He suggested that we should take him to Oklahoma City to Children's hospital.

Edgar came to the hospital and the older doctor was there checking on Matthew. I told Edgar what the young doctor had said, and the older doctor told Edgar that I was being a hypochondriac and that Matthew would be just fine staying at this hospital. Edgar sided with the older doctor and refused to take us to Oklahoma City.

The fifth day Matthew was in the hospital, he still couldn't eat and could barely talk. He had been given some Avon cologne and repeatedly used it that day. When I told him he needed to save some for another day, his response was I'll have enough. He also had been given a punch out of a shoreline and boats to color and put together. He worked very hard on it, saying I've got to finish this.

Then later that day Edgar told him he needed to get better because he needed to go back to Amarillo, and he needed a riding partner. Matthew loved to go with him and was always very quiet in court and everyone complimented Edgar on how well behaved he was. Matthew looked up at Edgar and said, 'I've already been there it will be ok.'

We all thought this was strange and wondered about the comment. That night Matthew begged for me to stay the night with him. He had never asked that before. Momma didn't feel comfortable going to my house without me there, so I got Matthew to sleep and then left.

Two hours later I got a call telling me that Matthew had awakened and was upset she wasn't there. I rushed to the hospital. By the time I arrived they were taking Matthew back to the surgery room.

That morning they poured sixteen pints of stored blood into him. I was told there was blood coming out of him every-

where it had an outlet. At first, I could hear him crying as I waited outside the surgery room. Then the crying stopped.

Soon the older doctor came out. The young doctor was standing beside me, and the hospital administrator was across from him. The older doctor told me that Matthew had passed away. I was so enraged, I lunged at the older doctor and blacked his eye. The other two men pulled me off him. I wanted to kill him at that point.

The older doctor told me, 'You have to pull yourself together, you have three other boys that need you.'

I asked, "What do you mean?"

He said, 'Look around you. Who is here with you?'

My mom was in the patient room and Edgar was asleep on the couch downstairs. I was all alone. He said, 'You're the only one who is strong enough to take care of your other children.'

I thought about what he had said, and thought I am all alone. No one cares enough to be here with me.

My father had left the night before because a church member was having surgery the next day and he needed to be there. Mom was not there beside me, instead she was in the patient room and Edgar, well he never had cared for me the way I should have been cared for.

The three men calmed me down and asked who they needed to help me call. Martha was the only person who would understand and help me. They placed the call to Nebraska where Martha was still asleep. She told me she was so sorry and would gather the family and they would be there as soon as they could drive there.

My younger sister, Lizzy, lived in Enid and would come as soon as she could get around.

I was allowed to view Matthew and say goodbye before they came and took him to the funeral home.

Edgar took me and Momma back to our house. They called the different family members when they got home. The outpouring from the community was unreal. There was so much food brought in that I didn't have to worry about feeding people. I just let everyone do as they pleased for food.

The hardest part was telling Terrance.

The other boys weren't old enough to understand.

CHAPTER 15

Burying a child and taking care of husband

Cia sat and thought about the horror show that had been her life until recently. The loss of her child was an event that caused her deep grief for years. As time went by, she felt the grief soften a bit, but it was always with her. The scars of those weeks and days would always be with her.

For a time, she went to Dale Carnegie with others in the clinic she was working with. After that Cia had coached with the class and one evening, the coach/teacher, asked her to give a speech on someone that gave her the strength to be who she was today. Cia had asked, "What if there was no one."

He told her there was something in her past that had made her the strong and courageous woman she was today. He worked with her for several minutes that night after class. Finally, he asked about trauma in her life. She told him about her child dying and about the older doctor. Cia fell apart that night and cried uncontrollably. It took her several minutes to regain her poise and calm. When she was able to calm herself, he said, "Just think about it and we'll work on it next week when you come to class."

The week passed quickly and when she got to class, he apologized for upsetting her. Cia told him it wasn't him that upset her. The fact of the matter was the person who took her son's life was the one responsible for her being strong. In those moments she understood the man she reviled the most, was the man who made her stronger. That realization was why she cried.

I remembered when Lizzy got to our house with her baby

daughter. Her baby had always cried when I held her. This upset me because I longed for a daughter to love and cherish. Lizzy said she needed to give her a bath and I asked if I could. Lizzy was reluctant because the baby loved her bath, and she was afraid it would upset her to have me bathe her. Lizzy stayed in the bathroom and when I was in the bathtub, she handed her daughter to me. I was able to relax and enjoy holding her. My niece could sense this and was very calm and enjoyed her bath very much. After the bath, for the rest of their lives, my niece and I were very close.

That evening, people came and went extending their condolences to me and my family. About that time the dreaded sister-in-law and mother-in-law pulled up to the back door. I was standing in the door and visiting with my next-door neighbor. When my sister-in-law got to the door, she shoved me to the floor and my mother-in-law hit me with her cane and was uttering mean words to me. The neighbor helped me up. My neighbor was very upset about it all. I explained that was what my life was like, and I had no control over when or where they would be rude or hateful to me. The neighbor apologized for their behavior.

The day of the funeral the sister-in-law proceeded to tell Martha in front of everyone that she was fat. I was so embarrassed. Martha took it in stride and did not cause a scene.

Several of my aunts and uncles were there also supporting me. I thought to myself, 'no they're here supporting my parents who were acting so distraught. It wasn't their child, it was mine. I'm the one with a hole in my heart.' I wanted to scream but knew it would not do any good.

The rest of the day was difficult. It was hard to believe my sweet child would never sit in my lap again. I missed him so much. It made my other children, even more dear to my heart.

Cia would suffer more abuse and continued to strive towards

her degree. Her goal for her life was to get her children and herself away from the abuse.

> The next day we drove to several homes delivering the dishes of food had been brought in. When we got to my sister-in-law's home, I refused to get out of the car. My sister-in-law came to the car and told me that it was for the best that Matthew had died. I was so upset, and I couldn't believe she had just said that. I hated being there in that moment. How can anyone be so insensitive? Thank heavens Edgar could tell I was at my wits end and excused us and we went home.

****

Cia sat in silence as she remembered about that time in her life. It was extremely difficult to move forward. She would never get over the loss of her child's life. Forty-four years ago, seemed like yesterday. All the emotions, the feeling of loss and the desperate desire to have Matthew back in her life, was still as raw and painful as it was on the day he died.

It was getting time for Thanksgiving and the dreaded holiday of Christmas. Matthew was born on Christmas day. Cia loved her decorations but had a hard time getting through Christmas day. She always wished things were different but on Christmas Day it was an open wound every year.

She sighed, opened her diary, and began to write again.

> Monday, please hurry up! I remember feeling exactly that way and nearly shouted those words. I needed to go back to work. I needed to be around people that wanted to be around me and not all this negative energy that has been filling me these last few days.

> My boss had told me to take as long as I needed, but I truly needed to be back around my clients and my boss. The first client that came in that day was a lady that enjoyed talking with me, but really didn't know me at all. The lady said to me, "Did

you hear about the young boy in Mooreland that died?"

I said, "Yes ma'am he was my son." The lady was very apologetic. I said, "Don't worry, you didn't know, and I am glad that people thought it was a tragedy, because it was."

The older doctor was run out of town shortly after this. There had been several older people from the nursing home that died either during surgery or before they could recuperate. The town was beginning to worry about his ability to do surgery. After a young child died, the community just could not cope with it.

The older doctor came to our home when he was getting ready to leave town and asked if we wanted to buy his home. I couldn't believe the jerk had the nerve to come and ask. There was no way in hell that I would have lived in his home.

Later that summer Terrance needed to have surgery on his heel cord. I insisted that he be sent to Children's for a second opinion. This time Edgar agreed that a specialist should be consulted. After meeting with a hematologist and an orthopedic specialist it was determined that the tight heel cord could be corrected with bracing and no need for surgery. The hematologist had informed Cia and Edgar that Terrance and Matthew had a blood condition called von Willebrand's. There wasn't a lot known at the time about this condition. They just knew that there were not enough platelets so the blood would clot and when injury happened in blood rich, soft tissue areas, which the throat is one of those areas, the blood takes a long time to clot. Terrance's clotting time was 14 1/2 minutes. If the injury happened where there was muscle it would help clot the blood faster.

In August, when classes resumed for the fall semester, I decided to take a night class. It was one night a week, and it would help me get my feet wet and back into the swing of going to college. That semester I was taking Tax Accounting. My pro-

fessor had taught the business law class I had taken earlier. Since I was working in a tax office and had taken a course about all the changes in the tax laws for that year, it was a breeze for me. In fact, my professor would ask for my help in class in describing what was meant and how to answer some of the class questions. This was a confidence boost for me and helped me to move forward in my career.

Edgar kept being sickly and did not have insurance. He needed to have heart surgery but could not afford to have it. He was born with a hole in his heart and had been told that he wouldn't live another 5 years in 1955. Well, here it was 1977 and he was still alive.

I knew that I was going to have to give up my job at the accounting firm and find a job where group insurance was offered so that Edgar could be covered. I went to work in the business office at the hospital in Shattuck so I could get family coverage on my insurance. After coverage began, Edgar was seen by a heart specialist in Oklahoma City. He was put in the hospital for a heart catherization to see if he had other problems with his heart besides the hole. There was some damage and they scheduled him for surgery.

Mom and Dad had the 3 boys and taking care of them. Terrance was in kindergarten, and he needed to continue school. The day before his surgery Edgar asked me to spend the day with my aunt in Oklahoma City. I was ready for a break from the hospital, and he was in good hands there. They could call my aunt's if there were any problems.

When I returned that afternoon, there were several people in the room and Edgar was signing some documents. I asked what was going on all Edgar said it was legal papers and didn't want to go into details. Edgar had his surgery the next morning and after 4 days of recovery they were ready to send him home. It was winter and it always snows when you don't need it to. Well, this day was no exception. We had had several days of snow, and I had to drive the 3 hours back to Shattuck. By the time we got to Shattuck, Edgar was running a fever and could not get warm. I called his family doctor and was told to take him to the emergency room. At the emergency room we were told he had developed pneumonia. Edgar was hospitalized again in Shattuck. I was told to go home and rest that he would be in ICU and there was nothing I could do at that point. I went home, because I was exhausted and had to get some rest.

CHAPTER 16

Edgar's Open Heart Surgery

Cia worked around the house a bit. Some of her friends were coming to tour the house later that afternoon. Cia decided to make some of her oatmeal raisin caramel cookies. They had become a hit with her friends. She loved cooking in her new kitchen. She'd never had an island and loved the way her mixer was hidden out of site until she needed it. It was a perfect height for mixing. She had plenty of room for the ingredients and working with doughs, or casseroles. After the cookies were finished and making sure everything was in its place, Cia went to the back porch with her Diet Dr. Pepper, fresh hot cookies, pen, and diary to continue writing.

> *The next morning, I was unpacking the things from Edgar's hospital stay. I needed to get Edgar's night clothes washed to take back to the hospital. When I opened the suitcase, I noticed the envelope that I had seen at the hospital. I opened the envelope and held the papers. It was Edgar's Last Will and Testament.*

> *I thought, 'this will show me how Edgar really feels about me'. I was shocked to say the very least when I read his will. He had asked the court to take the children from me, stating I was a horrible mother, unfit to take care of my children.*

> *I sat and cried, then started screaming. After a few minutes I was able to pull myself together and said, "You don't deserve my tears, you bastard, Edgar. You know my children are my greatest treasure."*

> *The mean sister-in-law was who he was asking the court*

to give custody of my children.

After me giving up my dream job and getting a job to cover his sorry ass made me really hate him more and more. I made up my mind that day: I didn't care what else was going on but I would go back to school and get my degree so I could finally be rid of Edgar.

When Edgar was released from the hospital, I did not bring up the will immediately. I waited for a few months. Edgar's heart was not in rhythm and in April of 1978 was told he would have to have his heart shocked to see if they could get it back into rhythm. Before we went to the hospital to have the procedure done, I finally talked with Edgar about the will.

I begged him to please change what was in the will. He refused. He had been too weak to beat on me, but he knew how to hurt me more than the physical beatings.

I took him to the hospital in Oklahoma City. He was in ICU again, which meant I had to stay in a waiting room most of the time. I was determined to not sit there wringing my hands over the man I loathed. I bought yarn and a book and taught myself how to crochet. I made a lovely afghan while sitting most of the day by myself.

Edgar kept asking the nursing staff what I was doing and asking if I could come be in where he was. When he would get upset his heart rate would escalate, so they began to let me stay longer times with him. I couldn't understand why he wanted me in there. He sure hadn't been treating me very well.

Finally, the day came for the procedure, and it was successful. After 2 more days for observation, Edgar was released to go back home. Edgar regained strength and was able to continue life like before his surgery.

It was time for Cia's friends to arrive, so she cleaned up her writing area and put things away. She was really looking forward to her friends coming.

****

Cia had enjoyed her friends. They had been very impressed with what she and Jock had done to the house. Cia loved her new home and the new life that she and Jock were creating for themselves. She gathered her Diet Dr. Pepper, pen, and diary and went to her favorite spot on her deck. She settled herself, listening to the soft splashes of her water fountain and began to relax. The memories came rushing back as she wrote:

I prepared for the fall semester at the University in Alva. I had taken over Edgar's tax clients and we decided to open a small office in downtown Shattuck. I liked it because I could do my homework in between seeing clients. The kids were either in school or at the daycare center. They loved the daycare owner. They were well cared for during the day, which gave me much more freedom.

I attended college 3 days a week. I drove to Woodward and met up with 2 other ladies and then we all continued to Alva to college. I would drive 95 miles each way to school. I took as many credits as was allowed each semester to make the most of my time at school.

Edgar always complained about how little time I was at home. I knew I had to do this to take care of my children. I also knew that one day I would break free. So, I worked hard, continued in school, and ran my tax and bookkeeping office. I kept a B average and felt good about that. Most of my classes I seemed to breeze through.

The more classes I finished with good grades, the meaner Edgar would become. He would fly off the handle and start hitting me for no reason. It became harder and harder to study. This is what he wanted, he wanted me to fail. My last semester in school I would have to stay at our pastor's home of an even-

ing until Edgar would go to bed. Then I would get my children to bed and study until 11 or so and then get up at 5:30 the next morning to start all over again.

I just tried to stay as far away from Edgar as possible. As I neared the end of my education, I had completed everything except for the second semester of business law. I just could not fit it in my last semester. I knew I would not be able to go back to school after that semester. It took me 10 more years before I was able to complete my degree, but I did complete it.

Cia thought back on the hardships she had suffered trying to get her degree. She wished her sons believed her about how hard life had been and how hard she worked to stay in school and complete a degree. They each one had been given a way to go to school without owing anything when they were through. Sadly, none of them completed more than one year.

CHAPTER 17

Starting a New Life

Cia looked around her wonderful new house. She noticed the shelving unit that Jock had built. Cia had showed him a picture from Facebook, he took it from there. They had several doors that were not used in the remodel. Jock hinged 2- 30-inch doors together and then he took 2–24-inch doors and hinged them to the 30-inch doors and created 3 shelving units. He made the shelves out of the trim that was not used in the remodel. Cia and Jock painted the shelves with the wall paint from inside. Jock used the door facings to create a bookcase and CD storage unit that they also painted like the walls. Cia looked in amazement at all the things Jock had added his touch too. She was so proud of what she and Jock had accomplished. She loved her back deck, it was totally relaxing and gave way for more memories.

I finished my last semester, and then Edgar and I separated. The divorce was not final, but I needed money, so I had to immediately start looking for a job. The oil field was booming at the time in Northwest Oklahoma. I applied for an office manager position at one of the oil field service companies.

During the interview I was handed a balance sheet and was asked, "Can you tell me where my money is for the accumulated depreciation?"

I looked stunned as accumulated depreciation was not money. It wasn't really a part of the balance sheet. It was just an estimate of the amount of use of the equipment. By the time I finished explaining accumulated depreciation to my future boss, he let me know I had explained it well.

He told me that his CPA had given him that question to ask so he would know the right person for the job when they could answer it correctly. He told me I was the last of 40 people that he interviewed for the job and was the only one who answered it correctly. I was hired on the spot.

My boss took me upstairs to my office and introduced me to my staff and told me 'Here is your desk, if you have any questions, please do not hesitate to ask.' My boss told me that my predecessor was 3 months behind on everything when I took over. He was sorry he couldn't tell me more.

I talked with each of the ladies who worked there and learned what each one did. There were 2 younger ladies that sat at the break room table, and I watched to see what they did. Finally, I asked one of the other ladies what they were supposed to be doing, she looked at me and said, "I don't know." I asked my boss. He said the previous manager had asked for more help, so those girls were to help make copies or whatever anyone else needed. I informed him that both of the other ladies had said they didn't need help.

He brought the girls back downstairs and put them to work down there. They weren't very happy with me, but I didn't care. I was still trying to figure out what I would be doing. I found a file cabinet and went through it and found several coupon books for payments to the bank. The prior 3 months were still in the books. I took the books down to my boss and he told me, 'I don't know, I haven't had a financial in the last 3 months or I could tell you if we were behind on payments.'

He turned to his phone, called his banker, and was told they were getting ready to come and repossess his property for lack of payment. He asked the banker if he didn't have enough money in his account to make the payments and was told yes you have more than enough. He gave approval for the pay-

ments to be withdrawn and brought his note payments up to date.

He then turned to me and said, 'I need you to work with our CPA. He will be here tomorrow to teach you what he needs done in order to get our financial statements caught up.

The next day we worked through the first one, and the CPA was impressed with how much I knew about accounting and how to prepare the statements. He left me with instructions for the next 2 months. He would be back in a week and asked me to have this work completed by the time he was back.

I loved the work and had accomplished it all. I even learned how to do payroll on the computer. The books were kept by hand. This was before computers were used in small office settings.

I continued to live in the home in Shattuck until the divorce was final. I changed the locks, hoping to be able to sleep without fear. However, Edgar was enraged I had changed the locks so he couldn't come and go as he pleased. One evening he kicked in the back door and proceeded to beat me again. I truly feared for my life.

When I went to work the next day, I had a black eye and a big bruise on my arm. I was new at the office and so everyone was afraid to ask what was going on. My new boss called me into his office and asked if I was ok. I told him what had happened and the circumstances of my living situation.

He told me that he was sorry and hoped I could continue to work. I told him I would be at work every day. The police had told Edgar to leave me alone. He was the City Attorney, so he wasn't charged with spousal abuse. The police told him he had to stay away until after the divorce was final and the judge would determine who would get to have the home. It was his before the marriage, so after the divorce I moved to Woodward.

It was closer to work anyway and it helped me financially a lot.

Edgar was required to pay me $20,000 as my part of the equity in the property he owned during their marriage. He was also directed to pay child support of $300 per month for his 2 children but nothing for Terrance who was from my first marriage.

Edgar was very upset about having to pay anything and was very verbal during the hearing and during the arbitration that the judge had ordered to happen. It was a long 8 months before the divorce was final. Edgar however would not leave me and the kids alone.

There was never any relief or being able to establish a routine. He would come by my home every evening and pick the boys up and take them home with him. He was always late at getting them to school the next day.

This continued for 2 years before I moved to Amarillo.

Cia closed her diary for the day. She was feeling proud of herself for getting away from Edgar and the abuse. She was so thankful that Jock was not abusive. He was a very loving and kind husband. She was truly happy.

CHAPTER 18

New Adventures

Cia helped Jock plant the new bushes that came in the mail today. There were 12 in all. They planted 10 ever blooming Azaleas. Some had come with blossoms already on them. Then they planted the 2 confederate Jasmine that would spread over the trellis. Cia loved how Jock was willing to help make the flower garden beautiful. He had already erected the stone hinge fountain. That was a task, but it was oh so awesome. They were working out the details about putting a smaller fountain in the back to help with the splash created by the water falling five feet and landing on the rocks below. Cia washed up from the planting, gathered her Diet Dr. Pepper, pen, and diary and headed to her favorite spot.

I moved to Vici, Oklahoma to be close to my parents so that they could help with the care of my children. It was a smaller town, and the boys could go to school there and walk to the grandparents. It worked out best for all of us.

I continued to work in the oil field. My parents were called to a church in Amarillo around 1982. They moved out there and I found care for my children. It wasn't long after they moved and got settled that the kids and I went for a visit.

The parsonage was probably the nicest home Momma had ever had. It was decorated beautifully as always. Momma had that touch with making things look good, even if the dwelling was below par.

When I attended church, I was surprised at the congregation. There were around 50 people or so that day. The service was nice. Up at the front of the church on the opposite side was a man sitting with his young daughter. He was absolutely gorgeous in my mind. In fact, I referred to him as a hunk. I tried to get around to meet him, but he was gone before I could make my way over.

When we got back to the parsonage, I asked Mom who the man was. She told me his name was Dugan Gallagher and his grandmother and uncle were members of the church. His little girl was 3, and her name was Adelaide, but they called her Addy. Dugan had had custody of her since she was 6 months old. Her mother was a drug addict with mental issues and could not care for her daughter. She spent most of the time they were together in a mental institute. I was told he also had another daughter by his first marriage. Her name was Ava Gallagher.

I decided I would put it out that I would be back in town the next Friday. If there was a way to meet him, I felt sure the universe would find a way. As it was, he had gone to his mother's home for lunch. He told her that he saw a lady today that was going to be his wife and help him with his daughters.

His mother laughed but things were put into motion. The next weekend Dugan came to my parents' house for dinner, and we were introduced. To say we hit it off immediately was an understatement. By Thanksgiving we were an item.

I turned in my resignation at my job and moved to Amarillo during the holiday. My parents' home had a large suite at the back of the house that had its own bathroom. I brought all our things and set up the space for us to live in. The boys' beds and my queen size bed all fit nicely in the room, and we had room to spare.

The next week I took my children to school. The school was just a couple of blocks from my parents' house. This was the first time that Edgar had not bothered me. He did not try to stop me from moving, which was a fear I had. I was far enough away that he wasn't constantly coming by the house and taking the kids.

I was able to establish routines with the children. Edgar then followed the court rulings for visitation. It was much easier for me, and I hoped the kids would adjust. For the most part they did, and I felt closer to them than I ever had.

I blamed Edgar for Matthew's death. I felt if we'd taken him to Oklahoma City to Children's Hospital, he would still be alive.

I went searching for a job and found one with a builder's company. Dugan asked me to marry him at Christmas time. We decided to get married at my parents' home on January 28th, 1983. We had a justice of the peace come to the house and marry us. Our children, all 5 of them, were there.

I had made matching dresses for the girls, and we had matching sweaters for the boys. Both sets of parents and the aunt and uncle that Dugan was close to were in attendance. There was also a couple from the church that stood up for me and Dugan. It was a nice short service.

Momma had made and decorated a small cake for the reception. Dugan's uncle took Ava back to her mother, and they kept Addy for the weekend. Dugan and I spent the weekend in Oklahoma City.

The next week we moved into the little house Dugan was renting from another church. It began to snow that Monday. By the time we drove across town with the mattresses, they were covered in snow. However, by the next morning we had 12 inches of snow. Our new little family was stuck in the house for a week. It had snowed more several times that week. Everyone came out alive, so we had passed our first hurdle.

Dugan worked an 8-5 shift at the Asarco in the warehouse. He was home every weekend, and I usually worked the same shift with my jobs. Dugan was active in church also which made me very happy. We worked with the youth, worked on bible quizzing and such. We took the kids to different towns for their competitions. Life was really good for me at this point.

I became pregnant in 1985 shortly after our second anniversary. We had recently bought a home. It was across the street from the grade school. There was a nice playground and the kids loved being outside and playing on the playground.

Caleb Gallagher was born Nov. 3, 1985, in Amarillo, Texas. I had been telling my OB doctor that I had never been awake during any of the deliveries of my other 4 children, during my whole time seeing the doctor. The day I delivered, the doctor was sitting at the foot of my bed and said, 'now what are you used to doing at this stage?' It was time to push. I reminded him I had never been awake before.

He suddenly heard what I meant. He said, 'Well we have some nursing students here today, do you mind if they help you through this stage?'

I told him no so the students, one of each side of me, started telling me about how to push when I had a contraction. I was so afraid of acting like a fool with the pain. I had been in the hospital with contractions 3 times before I actually was kept to give birth.

There was lots of screaming and yelling and I was sure hoping that wasn't going to be me. The doctor told me to relax, and they would get through this just fine. He said those are spoiled little girls that disobeyed their parents and never had a tough day in their life. I felt better because I had been through plenty of abuse.

When it came time to push Caleb started coming out. The pressure was intense as I remembered. All I could think was GET IT OUT, GET IT OUT!!!!!

Everyone in the room chuckled as I was not thinking those words. I was saying them out loud. Then the pain was over.

My precious little boy was on my chest, and I was kissing him, cooing to him and reveling in the joy of his birth.

The first thing Dugan said was "he has toes."

The doctor asked, 'what did you expect?"

Dugan answered, "nubs like his mother has." I was taken aback. Yes, I have short toes and short feet for that matter. But they'd never been called nubs. Kind of embarrassed me, but I decided to roll with the punches. After all it didn't include hitting her.

That evening my parents brought Addy, Terrance, Slade, and August to visit me and to see their new brother. They were all excited and eager to hold him. Addy was in the first grade by this time.

Two weeks after we got home, I got Caleb ready and took him to school as a surprise for Addy for her show and tell. The class was excited, and she was so proud to show off her new brother.

****

Cia thought about how proud of Caleb she was. Caleb had his issues growing up. Got into drugs and all kinds of bad behaviors. He met his wife while working at a restaurant. One evening they were counting their money and decided they had enough money to move to Dallas, rent an apartment and start a new life and get away from the drugs. Cia was so relieved. Since that time, they have given Cia two wonderful granddaughters and they are both in church. Caleb is a firefighter and paramedic and is currently going to school to become an RN. To say Cia is proud is beyond words.

CHAPTER 19

Ending of Marriage Three

Cia dusted the family photos on top of her baby grand piano. She loved playing the piano but not nearly as much as she loved her children. She was proud of each of her sons and daughters. All had grown up using their own interests and talents to build lives any mother would be proud of.

When she picked up the photo of her marriage to Jock, she smiled, thinking of how fun the wedding had been with family and friends. They married in the large space of an older church in Oklahoma City. Early in their relationship, they'd joined an English Country Dancing group in the same space they were married in. With all their friends and family surrounding them, they married, then danced and had a grand time.

She dusted the photo and frame and said, "Jock, I know I can't go back and change my life. I met you just in time to help me create the life I'd always wanted. I can't change the past, although it changed me. With your love and support I am becoming the woman I'd always wanted to be."

She looked around her new home they'd spent many months refurbishing. She chuckled, "All you naysayers who thought we were crazy to buy this house, you ain't seen nothing yet."

She sat down and played *His Eye Is On The Sparrow* and sang every verse as she played. Her husband Jock, stood by the hallway door listening and watching the woman he loved. Before she finished the song, he brushed away a tear and quietly went back to their bedroom.

Cia sat still and quiet on the piano bench and then whispered to herself, "Not every man is mean and brutal. I finally have the right man for me."

She stood up, closed the keyboard, and walked to the kitchen. She picked up her diary and pen, fixed a glass of Diet Dr. Pepper and headed out to the back porch to write some more of the story of her life.

My life with Dugan Gallagher, wasn't a bed of roses, but he was a good man and life was better than it had been. He was a smoker when they married. When their son Caleb was born, he had many bouts of illness. Finally, the doctor told Dugan as long as he continued to smoke around Caleb, his son would continue to have repeated illnesses.

He was determined to quit. He found some pills on-line that was supposed to help him quit smoking and they did. In 7 days, he quit smoking.

The house smelled much better and in a couple of weeks Caleb's lungs had cleared and he was a much happier baby. Life was good and continued to be better than I'd ever had until August of 1985.

Dugan was let from Asarco due to a reduction in force. He was given 2 weeks severance for every year he had worked there. It totaled 14 weeks. We had been talking of moving to Paris, Texas. He had family there and I had family there. We thought it would be nice to live somewhere other than Amarillo. We took this opportunity to move knowing we would never have this much money again.

Momma went with me to Paris to pick out a house. We settled on a 2 story older home. Momma helped me clean up the house which was really dirty.

The house was big enough for Addy to have her own room

and the boys to be spread out more. Terrance was able to have his own room. Slade and August would share a room and there was a separate room for Caleb.

Everything seemed to be going very well. I found a job immediately. Dugan however did not. He had his unemployment for 6 months but after that he didn't have anything coming in. He took care of the kids, so we did not have daycare expense which was great because I was only making $13,000 a year.

A year after being in Paris, Dugan finally got a job at Sara Lee bakery making bread. He liked it well enough, and the pay was better than unemployment. Still, it wasn't enough to support the family. When Caleb was 5, Dugan decided he would be a truck driver. He would be on the road most of the time.

He became very controlling and was furious if he was home and the family had anything planned. We never knew he would be home, and it was unfair to the kids to not let them be involved in activities.

Some of the things that infuriated Dugan was when Daddy became ill and had his open-heart surgery. Dugan felt as if I should be home cooking him meals instead of taking care of her mother and father. My uncle became very angry and threatened to go show him "How the cow ate cabbage" as they would say. Dugan kept calling and upsetting me at the hospital. I would just shake it off and go back to doing what needed to be done.

I took my parents to all their doctor appointments from 1992 through 2009 when I moved to Norman. Dugan was not happy with having me help my parents.

****

Cia sat in her comfy chair inside her new living room. Looking around she could see all the special touches, such as the family pictures of both her mother and father's families. She knew life was hard for them, but the difference between the two pictures was very surreal. Her mother's family didn't show that they were poor. They were well dressed, and lots of smiles. Her father's family showed they were poor. No smiles and anger filled their faces. She thought to herself, "no wonder dad never smiled, or laughed, he had a lot of hatred dished out to him." Even though dad may have had a hard time growing up, it did not excuse him from being so mean. Cia said to herself, "After all, life is what YOU make of it." Cia had tried her whole life to be better than what she had been shown. She just felt like life would be better if you were happier and more encouraging, instead of mean and tearing people down.

On February 4, 1995, I had to have a hysterectomy. I was having horrible periods and the pains were worse than when having labor with my children. It was difficult to work because it kept me with anemia, due to all the blood loss. Dugan was furious because I was having a hysterectomy. In the years that past he would become more aggressive, watching porn, and wanting to have sex more and more. He was very degrading to me and the "Want to have sex" was not there for me. He accused her of the doctors taking her "want to" out. It wasn't that at all. She didn't want whatever disease he might bring home and she was tired of being chewed at all the time. All I wanted was to be desired and loved like when we first met. I didn't want to share my husband with anyone else and I tried explaining to him that I needed to be treated better.

He would just scoff at me and continue to scream and yell at me. He never raised a hand to me, which I was thankful for, but words being said can hurt as much or more as the beatings.

Dugan started locking himself in a room and watching porn and then come out and expect me to hop to it. Well, that didn't set well with me. I knew we couldn't go on this way but didn't know what to do to fix it.

One day I had to drive him to the truck terminal 70 miles away. We had put his vehicle in the shop, and I had to have a vehicle to get back and forth. When we arrived at his shop, I could not wait for him to get out. I had cried most of the 70 miles we had traveled.

As I went back through Paris, I stopped at the beauty shop. I wanted a new style, including haircut. When I made it back to my Momma and Daddy's bakery, Mom asked, "What's going on?" She knew since I had done something different, and things were changing.

I told her I'd been yelled and screamed at for the last time. The next weekend when Dugan returned home, I told him I wanted a divorce. He was angry but left the house.

His first stop was a liquor store where he bought a case of beer and a carton of cigarettes. He was going to show me he could do whatever he wanted to do. Caleb and I lived alone at this point in time. Caleb was sad that his dad was gone but he was also relieved that the fighting had stopped. He was tired of seeing his mom so unhappy.

****

Cia was in her perfect new home and was eager to help Jock as they prepared a nice dinner for themselves and some of their neighbors. She was thankful that they had such wonderful neighbors and people who wanted to know each other more than just in passing. It was a fun evening with lots of laughter and joy. Cia's chili was a hit and her Oatmeal Raisin Caramel cookies were also.

CHAPTER 20

Dugan convinces another chance

Cia was thinking about the night before when she and Jock had hosted their first gathering in their new house. Jock was a little peppier this morning also. It feels good to make new friends and to have them truly interested in you. There has been lots of attention paid to us since we renovated one of the most beloved houses in Oak Grove, but to have friends that wanted to share our home was the icing on the cake.

I found a cheaper place to live, and we moved into a duplex. Soon one of her clients had a trailer they were wanting to sell, and they would carry the note. I moved into the trailer with Caleb. Dad bought the lot next to their house at a Sheriff's auction.

Caleb helped his granddad and another man clear the lot off. One of my clients had a business where he leveled land and also could bring in dirt. I contracted him to level the ground and to bring in a load of sand for them to move the trailer onto.

My parents helped me by paying for the utilities to be put in for my trailer. It had been raining for days which was unusual for the time of year. But finally, it was dry enough for my trailer to be moved in. I was so thankful it was not in the shipping yard anymore.

Daddy and I worked for about 6 weeks getting grass in my yard and building me a 30 ft walkway out of bricks. One of my friends made me a small bridge to go over the ditch in the front of my house so people could get from the road onto the walkway. This friend also built me a deck across the back of the trailer house.

It was a gorgeous setting and close to mom and dad. They would help with Caleb, although he was old enough to not need much supervision.

****

Jock had gone to Monroe and bought 75 bags of red hardwood mulch to put down in the flower bed. It changed the looks completely. After all the mulch was down, Cia placed some of her mom's figurines, including a carousel horse, in her flower beds. It gave a truly decorated feeling to the flower garden.

Jock's sister invited them to a Garden Club luncheon. They were both excited to go and meet more people in the town. Jock's sister brought a lady over and introduced them to her and she told them that their yard had been chosen for yard of the month by the Garden Club. Cia was thrilled. She had always wanted to be a part of such an organization and to have this honor bestowed on her was really exciting.

My home was lovely, but I was lonely. Dugan kept coming to ballgames and sitting with me to watch Caleb play football in junior high and on into high school. He would invite us out to eat. Then, suddenly his mom became very ill with cancer. Dugan spent the last couple of weeks of her life with her. I brought Caleb out to be with his dad for the funeral.

Around the same time Terrance and his wife, Auberta, were having a baby. She was older and the doctors knew it would be high-risk pregnancy. Auberta had bi-polar and was on several different medications. The month she became pregnant, her kidneys shut down. She had to go on dialysis. Auberta was hospitalized for most of the 29 weeks that she carried her precious gift. One morning when they checked in on Auberta the baby's heartbeat could not be found. They did an ultrasound and found that the baby had died.

We again rallied together to help with this. I told Dugan, "I just don't understand how we can be so good together in tragedy, but we can't be nice to each other while we're together." Dugan vowed that if I would try again, he promised he would be more understanding. He promised he would quit smoking. I finally gave in.

Caleb had gotten mixed up with drugs by this time and I was needing help with him. Dugan and I decided to remarry. Dugan bought a home in Powderly, Texas. Caleb and I moved in just before school started in August 2002. I had mixed emotions about moving back to the Paris, Texas area, but Dugan did not want to live in my beautiful trailer. In fact, we tried to get approval from the finance company to move the trailer over in the Paris area. I found out that they had not approved me buying the trailer from my client, as he had told me had been done. So all the money I had paid was lost and the finance company came after the trailer.

Well, you guessed it, Dugan didn't change. He continued to smoke in my house and everywhere. I became very sick with Chronic Bronchitis. The doctors told me it was because of the second-hand smoke. I would just barely get over one episode then have had another infection. I begged Dugan to quit smoking, but he would not.

The belittling and yelling at me continued and he spent more and more time on the computer watching porn. Then the Casino came to Hugo just outside of Powderly where we were living. The money we made went to the Casino and not to bills. Soon, I had nothing again.

Dugan was obnoxious to everyone including my boss. Then one day, he came into my office and slung a sheet of paper on my desk. He blurted out loudly, "The doctor said you need to have more sex with me, that would cure my problem."

My boss came into my office and asked Dugan to leave. He told him this was not the time nor the place for this kind of talk. After Dugan left my boss asked me how much I needed to be able to leave him. He said we'd work out a payment arrangement. He was about to leave town but didn't want to go unless he knew I would be ok. He told me to tell his son how much I needed and as long as he had the money in the bank it was mine.

I asked him to let me think about it and see. I wasn't totally ready to call it quits again. That night Dugan was so furious about being thrown out of my office and could not understand what he had done wrong. The more he complained the more I knew it was over.

The next day I asked for $2,000 so I could get an apartment and pay deposits. The check was written. I found a 2-bedroom duplex and put down the deposits. That weekend I didn't say anything to Dugan about my plans.

On Monday Terrance brought a friend and they helped me pack up my things out of our house. I knew I had at least 3 days before Dugan would be back in town. We moved everything on the inside that day and got it all unloaded in the duplex.

By nightfall I had my next house in order and felt very relieved. When Dugan called, I never let on what was going on.

Cia sighed, and thought to herself, "Man am I glad I don't have to worry about being treated that way anymore." Jock was so loving and kind. He loves me truly and deeply. It was natural and easy making a home with him.

CHAPTER 21

New Beginnings Life Alone?

Cia worked around her house for a bit. It was easy to clean, and she was so proud of her house and loved cleaning it. She wanted to keep it neat and tidy so that when the occasional person from town showed up asking about the house, it was not a fear of something being out of place. Cia and Jock loved showing off their new house and telling of its history.

Work was relaxing the next week knowing the burden of having Dugan around was gone. On Thursday of that week Dugan called me at work. He was going to have to do another run for delivery on Friday morning. He wanted to know if I would come out to his truck and get his check and get it cashed for him. I said sure and still hadn't said a thing to him about me moving out.

I took his check to the bank and cashed it. I drove to our house and put it on the kitchen counter along with my key to the house. This would be the last time I ever needed it.

When he got off work on Friday, he called me to let me know he was leaving Clarksville. I said, "Good deal," and hung up. I never answered my phone again that evening. Dugan called numerous times after he got to the house and saw all my things gone. He cursed and screamed and yelled on the messages he left, but I never responded.

The next morning, he called and left a calm message. He told me that we needed to talk and settle things. He knew he was wrong. He said I could claim anything for the divorce because whatever I said he had done.

This time I did not leave empty handed. I was awarded half of his retirement account. We met at a local restaurant and settled things as to who would get the home, it was in Dugan's name, so I was willing for him to continue with the home. I already had all the things I wanted from the home so there was no need to go over any of those details.

I informed Dugan that I purposely did not include Caleb in the move. He had not believed that Caleb was doing drugs, so I felt it better for him to deal with the issues that I had been dealing with instead of taking on that responsibility.

We parted as friends but knew we could never live together again. There was just not enough respect from him. I desperately needed respect.

****

Cia was sitting and getting teary eyed when Jock came up. He asked if she was ok. Cia shook her head and began telling Jock about what she had just written.

Cia said, "I was just realizing how hard it was to leave Caleb with Dugan when I left."

Jock pulled her close saying, "You did the best thing you could have done in the situation. Neither were respecting you at the time and you had to escape and live for yourself."

"You're right" Cia replied, "I'm just glad that Caleb doesn't hate me for it."

My life was leveling out and I felt more and more confident every day. I was loving being alone, probably for the first time in my life. No one was screaming and yelling at me, no one was telling me how awful I was. Cia had tried hard to please, but there is just no pleasing some people. She knew she needed to please her boss to an extent but not taking so much pressure from him also. They had a long talk when he returned from his fishing trip, and she let him know what bothered her about her job and he worked hard at making her feel good at her job.

Caleb called me and asked if I would go to a community theater production his friend was in. I agreed. It was nice being with Caleb without Dugan.

During the intermission Caleb said, "If you didn't want me living with you and dad, you should have just said so."

I told him, "I didn't want you and your drug buddies, nor did I want your dad living with me. I thought it best that I be the one to leave."

He said he understood. He was glad for his mom that she wasn't in all the turmoil. This was a building block for the rest of their lives and their relationship. Caleb and I were very close from this point forward.

****

Cia smiled as she continued to relive the time of growing and coming into her own. Some days, it seemed incredible to her all she'd done and lived through. She was prepping for dinner and making her favorite casserole. She said, "Well, Cia, even when your boss was preparing to sell his company you had new adventures ahead."

When she had the casserole in the oven, she sat at the kitchen island with her diary and wrote about the beginning of the best part of her life—but not without more drama and demands on her life.

Four months after I separated from Dugan, I received a call from my mother. Momma said, "We've used the last bit of our savings for your dad's insurance. I just don't know how we are going to make it."

They just didn't have much income. They were only receiving about $1100 a month. It wasn't enough for the medica-

tions, utilities, and food.

I was stunned and knew I would have to give up my freedom again. No matter how far I moved, it seemed her parents would always come near her. There were 5 siblings, but I seemed to be the one that was expected to take care of our parents.

I told Mom that I couldn't afford to live separately from them and help them financially. I offered to move back in with them and help with about $1000 a month for them. However, this time I put some stipulations on the move. I stated that I wanted the house free and clear. Her parents had setup a Trust a year or so back and, in the trust, I was given first dibs on the house, but had to pay my siblings the purchase price. My parents agreed and they actually followed through, which was a surprise to me. The first thing that I learned was that the house insurance had been canceled due to lack of funds. I immediately restored the insurance.

Jock walked into the kitchen and asked, "How's it going?"

Cia laughed. "The casserole is doing great. Me? I'm working on my emotional and psychological healing, but it's a tough slog."

Jock nodded. "I think you're doing great."

"Me too. I'll keep writing for a bit. Dinner will be ready in thirty minutes."

"Good. I'll go put things away in my workshop and then come help with last minute dinner needs."

CHAPTER 22

Moving Back Home

Cia had helped Jock clean up after dinner. She thanked Jock for helping with the clean up and then sat back down to her diary. She told Jock, I have a few more thoughts I'd like to get down before we relax for the evening.

I drove 45 minutes each way to and from work. I loved that alone time. It helped me relax and prepare for the different atmospheres at both locations.

Everything rocked on and was really going good for me. I had a very understanding boss who was willing to let me be flexible enough to take my parents to their doctor appointments. He knew that I would work hard and keep my work caught up.

Dad had really bad problems with his heart and had had multiple surgeries, including 2 open heart surgeries and 9 stints. Nothing was working. He was also having TIA's and was on lots of medications.

In 2007 he had a breakthrough seizure while getting up and going to the bathroom. He fell and hit his head on the bathroom counter. He was on blood thinners and blood was going everywhere. I was on the phone with 911 while Momma was holding a towel on the wound. The ambulance got there quickly.

By this time, he'd lost a lot of blood. The doctors stabilized him at our small hospital in Commerce and he was air-flighted to Presbyterian Hospital in Dallas. Mom and I followed in our car. By the time we got there he was already in a room. Mom and I had gotten a room in their hospitality section upstairs.

Martha and Lizzy showed up at the hospital. This was a shock as Martha had not been around mom and dad for about 20 years, or around me for about 16 years. I was glad they were there but was concerned. It all worked out.

Martha and Lizzy shared our room. It was like having a sleepover and we talked into the night and early morning. Lizzy shaved our dad the next morning and he bragged that he had been shaved by a doctor. Lizzy was an OBGYN by this time.

Dad was not going to be able to come directly home, he would need to go to a nursing home first. On the day he was dismissed from the hospital, he had another seizure going from his room to the car. I felt like we shouldn't take him but the nurse told me they had done all they could do for him.

After we got him to the nursing home, I knew things were much worse. Two days later we he had to be taken back to Presbyterian hospital. This time they kept him until he was more stable, and we brought him back to the house.

The next week Martha called me and asked if she could come for a visit. I told Martha if you are wanting to come back because you think dad is dying and there is money for you, you need to know there is nothing. Mom and Dad had nothing. The house has been deeded to me due to me helping them financially and as a caregiver.

Martha said, "I thought since dad was no longer physically able to hurt me, I would be safe to come visit. I really want to be near you and Momma."

After our 2-hour phone conversation I agreed for her to come visit. She came the next weekend which was Labor Day. She would be able to stay a little longer. Dad's brother also came to see him that day. Martha and I left the house and went for lunch so dad and his brother could talk.

It helped me to be able to be strong and stand up for myself. It was the first time in my life I had stood up for myself. I let Martha know what had upset me in the past and how I blamed Martha for my not getting to be with my high school boyfriend. Martha had no idea that dad had reacted like he did. It healed our relationship.

Cia sat and contemplated how things had drastically changed. She and Martha were closer than they had ever been. Cia thought to herself, "I think it is because I've learned the truth about our parents and how awful Martha was treated." Cia was glad she had let the barrier down and had agreed for Martha to come visit. Life would change for Cia after this.

Cia anxiously awaited when Covid-19 would get under control so that Martha and her husband would be able to travel and come see what she and Jock had created.

CHAPTER 23

Fixing up the parents home

Cia reread her previous entry about how she and Martha had become good friends. She chuckled and thought how she had hoped Martha might help her spread her wings and fly. That was exactly what had happened.

Cia had felt as if she would always have to live with her parents and not be able to do anything else. Having Martha back in her life changed all that.

She looked around the kitchen of her new home in Louisiana and knew, deep in her bones, that she'd never have gotten this far in her life without breaking the pattern of the constant need to care for her parents. *More importantly,* she thought, *I took the opportunities presented to me and climbed the ladder to my own personal and professional success.*

She finished clearing the table and counter-tops, filled a glass with ice and Diet Dr. Pepper and went back to the porch to write more of the new life she'd built.

> *I received my part of Dugan's retirement and wanted to make sure that the money did not go to waste. I bought a used Impala. That was the car my parents wanted. It wasn't the car I wanted but to keep the peace I bought the Impala.*
>
> *The house needed some tender love and care, so I put $30000 plus into the home. I had it leveled, put in new flooring, and painted and wallpapered throughout the house. My siblings each came and helped from time to time on the remodel. I knew this would come back to me when I later would*

sell the property. Keeping the home in good repair and ambiance would help me later get the best benefit from the sale of the home.

    Martha came to help with the renovation and talked with Daddy about how she felt he was weak enough he couldn't hurt her anymore. Daddy quipped back and said, "I guess I could smother you as you slept."

    I tried to get Momma to help us and make him apologize to Martha. Mom refused. I told mom that day from that point forward that I believed Martha and would stand up for her. Momma just stood there.

Cia sighed as she continued to reminisce about her life after Martha came back into it. It meant not only did she and Martha became good friends, but they became good business partners.

****

Cia remembered how Martha told her about her Nurse Practitioner clinic she opened in Norman in 2003. It was growing and Martha needed some help in auditing records, handling the financial side of the clinic, and making sure the front office was keeping things in order. Cia was excited that she could help her sister. Not only would she help Martha, but Cia would also give herself the possibility of moving forward in her own life.

    I would use some of my vacation time and spend it in Norman with Martha and her husband. We worked on the accounts receivable of Martha's business. I had become very proficient in working claims and it was easy to learn how to use their software. I felt as if I was really helping Martha. Also, it was really nice to have Martha in my corner.

    The first weekend the three of us found over $25,000 in claims that just needed a few corrections. I taught them how to work the claims in Soonercare and know that they were accepted.

I felt as if I was accomplishing great things for my sister.

In November of 2008, we three were eating dinner at an Italian restaurant. We talked about the possibilities moving forward for both myself and Martha. Martha asked me to come work full-time at her clinic. I told them they couldn't afford me. I'd audited their books and knew where things stood so wasn't at all sure the company could afford me full-time.

We talked some more, and Martha said, "We really need you at the clinic. We've talked about it and feel with you running the business side of things the clinic will bring in enough to pay you $50,000 a year."

I was stunned at the offer and said, "I'm making $36,000 at my current job. Also, I have concerns about taking care of Momma and Daddy."

Martha had a plan. She said I could do a lot of my work remotely from Mom and Dad's house in Commerce, Texas. We compromised that I'd work Tuesday through Thursday in Norman and Monday and Friday in Commerce. The plan allowed me to take our parents to their doctor's appointments.

I wouldn't have to move, and they said I could stay in their guest suite when I was in Norman. It seemed perfect so I accepted the position. It also gave me time to talk with my parents about moving to Norman. Moving made sense. I wouldn't have all the traveling could concentrate more on my job.

Of course, our parents balked at the idea. Momma didn't want to leave the house. I finally moved to Norman in March of 2009, leaving my parents behind.

I felt bad to an extent but also needed and wanted to be at the office more. Martha was needing a good business manager. My job would entail organizing the front office and help keep the finances in better control. Too many people were handling the money with little oversight.

I was surprised when Martha rallied the siblings and others would step in and help. I'd been providing the $1,000 a month I had promised our parents.

Martha took on the phone, cable and Internet bill which was around $300 a month and our older brother would send them $125 per pay period, which was around $250 a month. I sent them $450 a month. With all of us working together, I was able to have enough money to live in an apartment in Norman and go back to Commerce for the weekends.

Martha gave me my wings to fly when I was 57. It took 57 years for me to be on my own and have my own say so about my life. It felt so good to be by myself again. Martha bought me my first ever dog. Missy, a Havanese puppy. The breed was an allergy friendly dog that was good for apartment living. Missy was such a sweet dog, and we went everywhere together.

But I was also lonely. I still wanted a partner in my life. I went on-line and signed up to several dating sites. This proved to be somewhat troublesome. I didn't know how to verify that these guys were real and someone I would want in my life.

I remember the first guy. He was very nice. Martha and her husband meet him and liked him. After about 3 weeks, he suddenly began to act weird. Martha told me of a website to check out these guys. I was talking to this guy on the phone while I was looking on the website. It came up that he had been in prison for rape and kidnapping. Of course, I became alarmed and could hardly hear anything he was saying on the phone. I was texting Martha at the same time and asked her to look him up.

When Martha saw what I was seeing she told me to pack up enough stuff for the next day and come and spend the night with them. We would talk with her husband the next day. I got off the phone and packed hurriedly and went to Martha. All Martha said to her husband was that I had gotten spooked and needed to come over.

The next evening at dinner her husband asked me what had spooked me. I took a deep breath and told him what I'd found out.

"First off," he said, "I'm mad, he made me like him and I don't usually like people that quickly. Second, we're going to go with you to your house and get enough of your clothes for 2 weeks. I have asked for the house on Parkview as part of my inheritance from settling Mom and Dad's estate. My niece was living there but has bought a house and will be moving out soon. We can go in and make sure everything is ok for you to move in. This will be a new location so this dude should not be able to track you. Martha and I have been talking that this would be a good place for you, and we will carry the note on it, and you won't be just pouring your money down the drain."

It seemed like a perfect solution and again would help me move forward in life. The guy called that night and wanted to know why I sounded different on the phone. I just asked about the date on the report, and he said, "I was going to tell you."

My response was, "Sure you were. You should have told me before we ever met. That would have allowed me to make my own decision as to whether I wanted to meet you or not."

He agreed to never contact me again. I told him, "You ever contact me again you will be answering to the police."

He never contacted me again. Several months later another guy on the dating site started contacting through messaging at first and then started calling. You've probably already guessed, I was scammed big time, to the tune of about $3,000. It was a hard lesson, but one I guessed I had to learn. It was far too easy to believe someone when they said they liked you when you are lonely.

I gave up looking for several months. Then my baby

brother told me of a website called Plenty of Fish. This would prove to change my life forever.

Cia decided that enough was written that day about her past. She was so thankful for all that happened next in her life. Her children had become more active in her life, but it still wasn't the same as a life partner. She hoped that she could find the right person.

CHAPTER 24

Cia Invites Prince Charming Into Her Life

Cia grinned and reminisced about meeting Jock. She thought, *Life has been totally different since we met.* She loved Jock more than she'd thought she'd ever love anyone. They met on the website, Plenty of Fish. They talked back and forth through messaging. She found out information so she could look him up. There was nothing on the court sites except about his divorce. He told her he worked for Oklahoma University in the Rock Mechanics lab. She looked him up and sure enough there he was. She looked him up on-line and found that he had been published 25 times and had 6 patents at that time. He now has 8. She knew she would be safe in meeting him.

Jock and I set a date to meet. We were to meet at Charleston's, across the street from my office at 5 o'clock, July 19, 2010. I went early to watch him come into the restaurant. Little did I know he was already there. In fact, he had had a doctor's appointment at another doctor in the downstairs of our building.

We were led to a booth. We ordered our dinner and I wanted to prove I was an independent woman, paid for our dinner. I thought I'd shocked him, which I did.

We talked until after 9 that night. We both realized we had been talking and enjoying being around each other and had lost track of time. That was a Monday evening. He invited me to go to an English Country dance on Thursday evening with him. I was still a little leery and was not going to go hook line and sinker fast this time. Or so I thought—best laid plans and all that drivel.

Anyway, the dance was marvelous. I'd often thought I would have loved being born in that time. Jock stole my heart that evening. He called daily and we enjoyed just talking. He invited me for dinner.

After dinner, I wanted to continue talking but didn't want to show where I lived yet, so I took him back to our office. We sat in the waiting area and talked. I wanted to give him some of my past history. I told him that if he wanted to bolt now was the time to get going. I was falling and didn't want to be hurt again. Instead of bolting he invited me to a concert at "The Barn". One of the dance club members lived on a farm and a barn had been restored by the dance group as the dance barn where dances and concerts were held. It was a lovely concert, and I enjoyed every moment of the event.

I was becoming more and more attracted to Jock. On Friday of the second week, I offered to cook him dinner. I fixed him salmon, cherry pie and veggies. He loved everything. While watching TV that night, he asked me how I wanted the evening to go. I looked him in the eyes and said, "I bought a few special things for breakfast."

Their whole relationship changed in that moment. He jumped in just as deeply as I had done. We made love that night and became one. On Saturday he left to go mow his lawn and came back that evening. On Sunday he went to see his daughter.

I had a colonoscopy the next day, so I had the prep to do. Jock called me on his way back home and asked if I wanted company. I explained again what I was doing. He answered, "I know but thought it might be easier with company." What a way to get to know someone, right?

He went home about 9 that evening and I finished my prep. The next day one of my friends took me to the procedure. Jock came by around 4 to check on me and brought me egg drop soup.

Such a sweetheart. He showed up with his pillow the next night and he's been with me ever since.

When he talks about the past, he calls it his previous life—the life he lived before Cia. So sweet.

I went with Jock to his daughter's house for several weekends. She had 3 daughters. One Sunday we met at a Chinese food restaurant. After we filled plates and were eating his daughter asked, "When are you guys getting married?" Jock spoke up and said never. I was shocked. He went on to explain due to the marriage tax penalty we would not marry. His daughter was shocked also.

I spoke up and said, "Oh don't worry, when we get married, we'll have an English Country wedding and have a dance afterwards."

We just left the conversation at that. That night while in bed Jock said, "We could have our wedding in two weeks during the intermission at the dance".

I said, "Well there is just one problem with that".

Jock asked "What"?

I said, "You haven't asked me to marry you."

He was smart and quickly asked. Of course, the answer was yes. I told him 2 weeks wasn't enough time though. We were to go to meet his family. They were having a memorial service for his stepbrother who had passed away in May. The stepbrother's family would be there along with all of his other brothers and sisters. The sisters all had to talk with me to make sure I was good for Jock.

On our way back we were staying with my youngest brother. We went shopping for material for outfits for the wedding. After we arrived back home, Jock took me to the jewelry store, and we picked out our wedding rings. It was set in stone, so to say. The wedding would be happening.

I made my wedding dress, my matron of honor's dress and made Jock's English country outfit, shirt, pants, and vest. I also made a vest for the best man, Jock's best friend. Martha and her husband came from Washington. Her husband walked me down the aisle and presented me to Jock.

It was marvelous. We had our first dance and then we broke for the reception. They began again with a great march. This allowed Jock and me to be with everyone. Then we had a family and friends' dance. The dance was followed by 2 hours of dancing and merriment.

It was the grandest night I could ever imagined. I was flying so high that night. One of the band members asked if she was a happy as she seemed on the dance floor, and I said YES with great excitement. The band had made the event even more wonderful and soon we all became great friends.

Jock and I were dancing fools. We went to every dance and became very involved with the group. I knew I had found my perfect match. Love abounded and we grew closer together.

Cia decided that she needed to go see her therapist again. She was feeling the need to discuss this happier part of her life. Sandy Carver was excited when she read how Cia had stood up for herself and finally became her own person.

She knew that somewhere Cia had found the strength to give up on the abuse and not accept it again. Sandy said, "Your visits with me started out to uncover your childhood memories. That didn't really happen."

Cia nodded and said, "I'm no closer to remembering my childhood but I've begun to come to grips with it all. I realized the memories may be too painful to remember. I'm happy now and content."

"I'm so glad. So do you think we've come to an end with the counseling?"

"Yes, I think so, but I want to remain friends."

Sandy nodded. "Me too. I want to watch you continue to thrive in your new life."

CHAPTER 25

Cia Builds a Life of Love and Belonging

Cia sat on her screened in porch. She looked around the yard. Jock was laying the new grass sod after all the lawn was torn up during the rebuilding of their house. She smiled, knowing whatever she wanted, and he could accomplish, he would do for her. She'd never felt that sort of love or security.

Every time she looked at Jock, she felt a little thrill of joy and love. The past eleven years of her life had been wonderful. She was thankful to have met Jock and truly loved their life together.

She picked up her pen and diary and began writing about their early marriage.

> *Jock and I lived in the Parkview house after our marriage. We knew we would eventually need a bigger home. We wanted to have the spare home in case my parents decided to come to Norman in the future.*
>
> *In January of 2011 we moved into a home on Carolyn Court we bought from one of my partners in the nurse practitioner clinic. We rearranged and remodeled the kitchen but kept the cabinets to remodel the Parkview house with.*
>
> *We thought we would have a project to work on over the summer. Well as usual, our time-line didn't work out. We rushed to get it ready for my parents. On Monday after Mother's Day 2011 Mom called and wanted to know exactly how much it was costing me for them to live in their home in Commerce. I explained that I was giving them $450.00 a month and also paying the house payment on Parkview until they were ready to come to Norman. Momma said, "Your dad*

wants to be there around his kids before he couldn't remember things anymore."

His mind was slipping, and it was hard for him to remember everything. I immediately got out my graph paper and start planning for the Parkview house. I had to giggle because the boys hated seeing the graph paper come out. It usually meant they would have to move furniture. I began drawing out the dimensions of each room. I taped them all together and then we started the remodel process.

We decided to raise the floor of the one car garage, as my parents would not need a garage. It would be safer to not have steps to come up and down on all the time. That would also bring the washer and dryer to the level of the rest of the house. Mom could stay inside while she was doing laundry.

We could then close off the door in the kitchen going to the garage. We made a window where the door was going outside. At the front of the garage, we made a doorway coming into a ramp and leveling off just before where the washer and dryer were. We enclosed the rest of the front and put exterior siding across where the garage door had been.

In the kitchen we made a galley style kitchen with a peninsula going into the space where the small dining room had been. We took the wall out of the dining room going into the smallest bedroom to make a big dining room. My parents would have more people eating there than sleeping there.

We totally tore out the bathtub/shower and replaced all the fixtures in the bathroom. We installed a corner walk in shower and the toilet on one wall and a pedestal sink. This made it so if they had a walker or wheelchair, they could get close to the sink.

We also opened the tiny bedroom, now dining room, to the living room and put an opening from the living room into the *old garage, now a great room. We only had about 6 weeks to get this all done.*

The house was not completely ready, but Mom insisted on coming and helping with the remodel. All was ready except the great room needed wallboard, painting, and laying of the indoor/outdoor carpet that we had picked out for this house. The rest of the house had nice wood floors that we kept intact. We laid a nice linoleum in the kitchen.

We were very proud of what we'd accomplished. Moving day came and Martha and her daughter came to help us move mom and dad. We brought our pickup. Caleb and his wife came to Commerce and helped there. They also came to Norman the next day and helped unload the rented moving truck.

There were several of the church folks in Commerce that came and helped to finish the packing and loading the truck. Jock was in charge of packing the truck. One of the people said he'd never seen a truck packed as tight as Jock had packed that truck. The back of Jock's pickup was full of things that would not fit in the truck.

Martha's vehicle was for mom and dad. Martha's daughter road with me in the pickup. Jock drove the rented moving truck. After an eventful day the crew finally made it to Norman. Cia's oldest brother and some of his sons came to help with the unloading, along with Caleb and his wife and Martha and her daughter. It didn't take nearly as long to unload as it did to load. There was lots of fun and laughter. I was relieved to have my parents in the same town where we lived.

There were long nights and weekends of work still required to get the other areas of the house completed.

Cia looked around her new home and could see part of her mom in her house. She had acquired all of her mom's things when she went into a nursing home, as none of her siblings were interested in having mementos of their mother . The ceramic dolls that mom had worked so hard for were front and center in her living room. She placed them under her couch table, end table and on chairs and benches. Cia loved looking at them and reminiscing of how her mom had made all the gorgeous clothes that the dolls were wearing. Cia was proud to use them as part of her decorations in her home.

For the next couple of years, we hosted various get together with families. Mom and Dad had also had several parties and holidays at their house. Finally in 2013 we had completed the renovations of his home in Duncan from his previous life. It was ready to go on the market.

Jock had landed a much better job with Chesapeake Energy. We decided to find a bigger, nicer home. We were going to put their current house on the market, but it was not a good time to sell, so we rented our house to one of my employees.

She and her children were good tenants and kept good care of the house. Several years later when they were ready to move the market was better and so we put the Carolyn Court home up for sale.

The house on Ladbrook was supposed to be our forever home, but as time goes, things change.

Over the next year or so we had built a playground for our grandchildren. This was something I'd had always wanted for my boys but never had the money to do for them. I was thankful my business, the clinic I'd bought from Martha, was doing well. I was able to pay for the new playground. The grandchildren loved it, especially August's son and daughter, who assisted in leveling the ground where the playground equipment was built.

Cia looked out at the yard of her new house. She loved the green grass. The sod had taken well, and it had already been mowed a couple of times. The flower bed was gorgeous, and the fountains were always so nice to listen to. It was a very relaxing home. Cia and Jock were very happy with what they had created.

In August of 2014 there was more change coming to our home. My oldest son was in a relationship with another woman, Auren Dubin and had a baby with her. My grand-daughter's name was Candace Gallagher. Candace was 10 months old. Her half-sister Chloe Dubin was 11 and had been having behavioral issues for quite some time. Terrance called me and stated they were dismissing Chloe that day and if some-one in the family didn't come get her that the state would take custody of her.

Jock and I drove from Norman, Ok to Abilene, Texas to the behavioral health center and picked up Chloe. We had only had interactions with her a year earlier for Christmas. After we picked her up, we drove from Abilene, Texas to Amarillo Texas where Terrance and her mother were living.

During our travels that day we were in contact with De-partment of Human Services for Texas. They were forcing Ter-rance and Auren to move from their current location as the people they were staying with had records and could not stay there or they would be taking both children. We talked with their case worker, and they agreed to let them move to Norman.

We were not financially able to rent them a place to live and pay for everything. Neither Terrance nor Auren was work-ing. Auren was into drugs, and I knew the girls needed taking care of. Terrance was born with cerebral palsy, and I knew he mentally was not capable of taking care of his family. He could work if he wanted to, but most of the time was willing to just sit around.

So, our quiet home soon became filled with fussing and fighting. Something neither of us wanted. We felt we had to help the girls and didn't know what else to do.

Chloe was a troubled child and acted out to get attention. With the new baby in the house, it was hard for her. Her mother also was not capable of giving the kind of attention that Chloe needed. She tried being a friend instead of mother until she was mad and then the discipline did not fit the problem.

There were a couple of stays at rehab centers in Oklahoma for Chloe, but she had already learned the system and was out in a few days. She knew what to say and how to act. We were at a loss for how to cope. We wanted our peaceful life back.

Cia thought back about those times and wished she could have helped Chloe, but Chloe was not ready for help. Cia took a deep breathe and thought, *We'd of never been able to have done what we've done if Chloe was still in our custody.*

About that time Jock came bouncing onto the deck.

"What ya doing?"

Cia replied, "Just finishing up for the day in writing. I have a pot of cheesy chicken soup. You getting hungry?"

"You know me, I'm always hungry and especially for your cheesy chicken soup."

Cia closed up her diary, picked up her things and they went into the house to finish fixing dinner.

CHAPTER 26

Cia's Next Big Burden

Cia kept thinking about the past and what all it entailed. She was so thankful life was not like that now. Despite her son and his trials and tribulations with his children and wife, she was happy during her time in Norman, Oklahoma. But that was just the beginning of her happy life.

Now, she felt blessed with her Louisiana life and her newly refurbished home. Both she and Martha loved Craftsman style homes. That she and Jock had the opportunity to refurbish a for real mail-order home from the beginning of the twentieth century, was a real joy for her. Her home was everything she'd dreamed it would be.

Sitting on the screened in back porch she remembered her next big burden in her life before Louisiana. Once again, she'd been saddled with her parents and their needs.

She picked up her pen and diary and began writing the events of late 2014.

> *In October of 2014, I learned Daddy was falling a lot at their home. Mom had called me several times to have Jock help him into bed. They had even called 911 to get help for him.*

> *We knew it was time for my parents move in with us, but what about the other four who were already living with us? There just wasn't enough room. Also, I wasn't willing to subject my parents to the chaos that had been my home since my son and his family had moved in.*

> *I started looking for ways to resolve this issue. I was*

telling my hairdresser the circumstances. I knew I didn't want Terrance and Auren in the Parkview house because I knew they would not take care of it. The hairdresser asked what we wanted for the house, and I told her. She asked if we would consider carrying the note for her. We didn't know her very well but felt like this would be a great thing. After all, she was offering a three bedroom, two bath mobile home as trade-in on the Parkview house.

This would solve the issue for Terrance and Auren. All they had to come up with each month, was their utilities and a $250 lot rent. So in a matter of three days, we packed up everyone from both locations, got Terrance and Auren's things from the storage and made the mad dash house move.

During the packing and moving Jock was taking up carpet and putting down laminate flooring so dad wouldn't be sticking to the carpet, and it was much safer for him.

I hired Auren to help with my dad and she could continue her studies at the house and Candace would still be around every day. Chole was in the 7th grade and in school daily, so it was a win-win for everyone. I was still able to go to work and take care of my business. I felt like Mom and Dad would have the kind of help that they needed.

At first Auren was upset with me because I didn't let them move into the Parkview house, but later understood why the trailer was the best option for them.

Everything was going well with everyone until in March of 2015. Dad fell in the den and broke his hip. He had to undergo surgery. He had surgery on Friday of that week and Sunday during his therapy, he had a breakthrough seizure which virtually fried his brain.

He could not swallow at that point and went through therapy at a nursing home. He had two hospital stays during *the next month until the final one when he was put on Hospice. He could not move his head or swallow anything at this time. We kept him as peaceful as we could and watched him pass on April 5, 2015. It was a very peaceful passing and on Easter Sunday.*

Mom continued to live with us, and we enjoyed her company very much. She piddled around the house while we were working, and she loved working in our flower beds. She always kept them very nice. We had several house keepers, but mom wouldn't let them do a lot of cleaning.

February of 2017 both Mom and I became ill with the flu. We both had our vaccines but were very sick. Mine held on longer than Mom's. I was so weak I couldn't care for Mom. I asked my brother to step in and help with Mom. He took mom to his home and kept her until she fell in November of 2019.

She broke her pelvic and her S1 and S2 and the socket of her left hip. They did surgery on mom and left a bleeder and she lost half of her blood the first night. She recovered but lost use of her left leg. She has trouble remembering things but otherwise is doing very well. She knows who we are but anything recent she can't recall. It's sad, mom doesn't seem to be there at all. It is hard to visit even though I try.

Cia sat quietly thinking about what she had just written. Cia knew that her mom was in the best place for her. She couldn't lift and tug at her mom, and her mom is too weak to take care of herself. Cia had made peace with leaving her mother. She would visit as often as she could, but this time in Cia's life was for her and Jock.

CHAPTER 27

Cia Longing for Retirement

Cia sat and shook her head and wished she could have made things different. However, she knew she couldn't change the way things turned out. She felt a strong need to keep herself whole and moving forward. She chuckled a little, and muttered, "If for no other reason than to keep my sanity."

She walked around the yard a bit then went back to the porch and wrote again in her diary.

I continued to work at the clinic in Norman for the next year. Covid-19 hit, and I really could not take the risk of getting ill. So, I seldom went into the office, and worked mainly from home from January to August of 2020. The more I was home and not dealing with the everyday running of the clinic I realized it was truly time for a change.

Christmas of 2019, we had spent the Christmas holiday with his family in Kilbourne/Oak Grove area of Louisiana. For four days I was able to visit with Jock's family and became very close to them. They were all as friendly and loving as Jock had been. I longed for that.

I'd become very tired of dealing with people, employees and others who just didn't care. I hadn't found a church where I was happy and felt welcomed. I didn't have the encouragement I needed from my family or from my work family. I knew it was time to retire. I'd thought I'd probably work until I died.

We talked about my feelings a lot. Jock could retire also in January. So, we talked to our business partners about buying us out. They agreed to put together an offer and we would sit down and discuss. We decided to go to Kilbourne in October of 2020 to see about finding a house. We wanted to have a home base but really wanted to be able to travel.

Cia had always longed to live in a small, close-knit community. Cia loved that most everyone knew everyone, and also the fact that Jock was kin to a lot of the community. It was easy to get accepted to the community. Maybe because they had remodeled a dearly loved home, but also because the community welcomed new people.

We looked at 7 properties, but I fell in love with a 1913 Sears and Roebuck kit home. It looked in fairly good repair. We thought we could probably do about $100,000 renovations and have a nice home. There was also enough property to build a big 20 x 31 feet garage. It would be big enough to house the travel trailer we planned to purchase. Later Jock would also have a place to store his tools and piddle around in.

When we got back to Norman, we continued to talk with our business partners. The partners decided on an amount that they would be willing to pay us for our shares of the business. It was a little less than I felt it was worth, but it was still good enough to do what we wanted to do.

In November, we put in an offer with the bank which had repossessed the property. We were able to buy the property for $28,000.00. In the middle of November, we met with an inspector and found that the foundation was going to need a lot of work. We were still determined to refurbish this property. In December we hired a general contractor to oversee things and their team would start the repairs.

They brought in dirt to level up the area for the garage. When it was finally dry enough to pour the foundation for the garage, the building company went to work on preparing the building for shipping. Our dreams were coming together. I resigned effective January 1, 2021. Jock was waiting for his long-

term bonus to be paid. He had also told his supervisors that if a layoff was going to happen, he would like to be considered so that others could be spared. In early February Jock was laid off with a very nice package. It was better than just his long-term bonus.

The next chapter of our life was on the horizon.

Cia and Jock just had some of their new friends over to the house. They loved having people over. Cia loved telling how she and Jock had met and get to know the people that Jock had grown up with. He had been away for 45 years, but a lot of the people still remember him. As people get to know Cia and her background, they are encouraging her to write her story. They feel that there are lots of women who need to hear that there is life after abuse. Cia sure hopes that this will help others.

CHAPTER 28

Renovation: Building Dreams

Cia and Jock bought a travel trailer and new pickup to pull the trailer. On December 18th, after the Christmas party at her office, they headed off for their next adventure.

They drove to Oak Grove, Louisiana. It was a long trip, but they were excited to get the ball rolling for the start of their new life. They drove all evening and into the night. It was nearly midnight when they arrived in Oak Grove. It was the first night in their new trailer.

Cia and Jock both thought it was a wonderful experience. The Town of Oak Grove had a nice trailer park with electricity, water, and sewer hookups. In their trailer they used propane for heating and cooking. They didn't stay long this time. It was mainly a trip to get the trailer to Oak Grove so it would be available for them as they commuted back and forth between Norman, Oklahoma, and Oak Grove, Louisiana, getting their new home ready to live in.

They were back to Norman for Christmas and luckily had Candace for Christmas. The holiday was fun and filled with love and family. After the holiday, they decided to go back to Oak Grove in Cia's car. They took Candace home then hit the road again. Both Cia and Jock loved driving and traveling so enjoyed heading back to the house in Oak Grove eager to get started with the renovation.

First, they pulled out the carpet. Sadly, with the carpet gone it was evident the front room floor was rotted, and they couldn't salvage the oak floors. They talked with the general contractor and signed the contracts. The contractor's crew would begin tearing out walls immediately and then work on the foundation until Cia and Jock could return in March.

After Jock was laid off, they were able to put a rush on the details in Norman. They listed their house for sale and eagerly waited for the perfect buyers to want their home in Norman. They didn't have to wait long. It sold in less than two weeks.

Suddenly both Jock and Cia felt the rapid reality of their endeavor. The packing went into full swing as they went through all their belongings. They knew they had to get rid of a lot of things. However, no matter how much they decided to not take with them, it was not enough.

Kathryn, Cia's cousin, wanted to come and see their house in Louisiana. Cia was glad to have her along. They talked and reminisced and it all helped to keep Cia awake. While she drove her car, Jock drove the pickup and pulled the travel trailer back to Oak Grove after having some repairs on it.

They needed to leave Jock's pickup in Oak Grove so they would only have one vehicle to tow when they moved. In early March, they spent several days in Oak Grove checking on the progress of their home. They even went to Laurel, Mississippi in hopes of seeing Ben and Erin from HGTV. They visited their shop and bought some mementos.

When they returned to Norman, they rented their first moving truck, got it loaded and headed out the next morning to drive to Oak Grove. This time they were towing Cia's car and dogs. The dogs, Cia and Jock all rode in the moving truck. It was a really long drive. It seemed a lot longer than it had been before. They arrived late that night, exhausted and ready to settle in a bit.

To add to their fatigue, they realized the propane tanks were empty so there would be no heat in the trailer that night. They slept in their clothes with all the covers they could find and were barely warm. Jock never really got warm that night.

Cia posted on Face-book they were moving into town and would need help on that morning at 9 a.m. Rafi James was one of the young men that showed up to help unload the truck. He worked very hard, and Cia and Jock decided to ask if he would like to come back with them to Norman to help load the other truck. He was not working at the time and gladly accepted the work.

Cia, Jock and Rafi loaded up in Cia's car and headed back to Oklahoma to get the last load. They left their dogs with a groomer, so they could get a haircut and bath. Rafi helped Jock unload the storage buildings at their property. They were filled with Jock's tools, ladders, and sundry things any man who loved working with his hands would have. They worked 3 days packing at least 10 hours a day. Rafi worked hard with Jock and his work made Jock's life a lot easier.

When they had packed up everything, the next morning they all headed back to Oak Grove. Rafi drove Cia's car back. All the traveling had been hard on Cia. Her arthritis flared up leaving her in pain. It was a relief for Cia to have someone to drive for her. After talking with Rafi, she realized that he was close to Caleb's age.

> *I took out my diary and wrote about my feelings of leaving my lovely home and going to a home that was totally torn down to the studs. I suddenly realized that this was how mom must have felt when she left her home in Commerce, Texas.*

> *I also thought about all the times that my children had visited over the last 7 years. I soon realized, my children nor Jock's, hadn't really visited that much. Our grandchildren, on the other hand, had visited a lot.*

> *We loved our grandchildren very much, but we still missed the visits from our children. It would have been nice to*

have played games and gotten to know their interests and visions for their futures. Something that I had longed for. I felt used and like I was only good as a babysitter and not from a mother that they were proud of.

We had had girls' weeks with the girls. The 4 boy grandchildren were too scattered to do the same for the boys.

We also had Candace every other weekend and every Wednesday. Terrance would come for a bit each time but never for the whole time that Candace was at our house. I felt like he needed to step up and become a true father to Candance. I felt if we stayed that would never happen.

She closed her diary and watched the trees, creeks and hillocks passing by. She was eager to be back in Louisiana. When they arrived back in Oak Grove, Rafi told them he felt honored to have met them and would love to stay in contact. There was lots of work to be done and when Rafi was not working elsewhere, he was at their new home working with them. He finally found a good job but stayed in contact with Cia and Jock.

Jock made another trip back to Oklahoma to get the last bit of things he could pack in his truck and to make sure that the cleaners had come and cleaned the house.

On March 25th they signed on the sale of the house they'd lived in for many happy years. It was officially not their home anymore.

While Jock was gone to Oklahoma, Cia took this time to reassess her diary. She wanted to be able to lay to rest the insecurities and hurt from the past. She wanted to put a bow on it and call it finished.

I want all of my family to know the things I've written in my diary are true to the best of my knowledge. I love each one of my children and grandchildren. I also need to say I was very lonely in Norman. I needed companionship with my children.

I needed to know I was loved by them. Yes, Jock loves me and shows me his love daily, but there is more to my family than Jock. I do not regret taking care of my parents and know this was the right thing to do. I know mom is in the best place possible. She is safe and well cared for. I do miss her bright feisty spirit.

I don't want anyone to blame Jock for the move to Oak Grove, Louisiana. That was 100% my idea. It floored Jock, but after visiting with his family in 2019 I felt more a part of a family with them than I had in a long time.

I'm looking forward in my life. I hope at some point my children will have the same longing that I've had and want to be a part of my life. I cannot put my life on hold waiting for the possibilities though.

I love my brothers and sisters and will do anything within reason for them, but again I am living for me. I'm making my own way and finding a place where I belong. Where I can be respected for me and others not controlling my life.

Cia closed her diary, sighed, wiped the tears from her face. She said to herself, *I finally did it, I've let people know I was hurt, not by words, but by being ignored.* She got up, walked around her yard, and let out deep breathes, and was ready for the new life that she and Jock were creating.

CHAPTER 29

Graduation and Rennovations

Cia and Jock made another trip back to Oklahoma on May 13th. This time they stayed with Kathryn. She loved having company, and it was even her birthday. She cooked several meals for them and even bought herself a birthday cake.

They celebrated her birthday in high fashion and loads of joy. They felt like young kids. The laughter was contagious, and the friendship was even better. The next day they drove out to Shattuck, Oklahoma for Cia's oldest grandson's graduation.

Kathryn was a very good host. She took it in stride with her usual happy grace when Jock and Cia arrived back at her home at midnight. It was a very exciting time for them all since Kathryn was going to return to Oak Grove. This time she was able to stay two weeks. She wanted to help with sanding of trim and spend more time visiting.

Kathryn and Cia became very close during these visits. Cia felt as if she had another sister. Most of Kathryn's immediate family were deceased and she really didn't have anyone except her children. Cia was really needing a close friend and Kathryn filled the bill.

When they returned to Oak Grove, the plumber and electrician had gotten the water and electricity ready so that they could move the trailer from the RV Park to their new home. Jock wasn't sure about moving the trailer, but Cia and Kathryn were able to convince him to move the trailer to the house. A load of gravel was ordered, and a nice pad was made for the trailer. It made life much easier for them all. They were able to watch the progress of each step in the renovation of their new home.

Cia was glad they were there to oversee things. They made steps coming off the ramp so that if you were coming from the trailer you could come up the steps to get onto the back deck. We had a twelve-feet by thirty-six-foot back deck built. We also had it screened in so in the evenings we could spend time on it without having bugs biting us all the time. They built a five-foot ramp coming from the sidewalk we had poured. There was a four-foot landing and then a screen door going into the back deck. The deck was not enclosed until most of the walls were built, and cabinet work done. This was to avoid damaging the screens on the back deck.

The wall behind the fireplace and the dining room bay windows had to be totally replaced. Cia was amazed as she watched the contractors tear out the walls and put them back, usually in the same day. She was glad she was on site. Usually when she would go in, she would have them change something that had not been gone over with her. After a few days of this, one worker or another would say, "Here comes the boss." Cia had been told that you had to watch because they would do things like what they wanted and not necessarily what you wanted. She watched closely, not because she wanted to be bossy but because she wanted her dream home to be exactly how she had dreamed it would be.

She spent many hours picking out the flooring, paint colors and counter tops. She made color boards, took out the dreaded graph paper, sketched and studied and sought for hours on end to find the perfect interior design elements she longed for in her dream home. She wanted the home to be modern in use, but to seem as if it was from the same time-period when it was originally built.

Cia found tiles for her kitchen back-splash like ones she had seen in the early 1900's interiors. She also found a similar wallpaper for her small bath. She knew because it was so small the details and wallpaper would help make the room look bigger.

She felt as if remodeling and figuring things out was part of what she was becoming. She'd always had her mother's sense of making a home lovely, but now she felt it even more strongly. The feeling of being totally in sync with her home and how her efforts were making the home more beautiful was very gratifying. The contractors soon learned to ask questions instead of just doing. Asking her what she wanted made for happier work environment.

There were problems getting the electrician and the plumber working together and doing what they needed to do in a timely fashion. This probably added at least six weeks to the time-lines Cia had expected from the early estimates.

This was the first time in Cia's life that she truly felt in control of the situation and doing things that made her happy. Being true to herself. The more the house progressed the more pleased she was with her decisions and the better the house looked. Dealing with contractors and their attitudes was nothing that Cia hadn't experienced. However, this time she stuck to her desires and was true to herself in ways she hadn't done before. This time, she was the one paying the bills and if they wanted her money, they would build her home to her satisfaction.

She argued with the painter, electrician, and plumber. She even argued with the contractor wanting to put things other places than what she had designed. She had given them the designs and expected them to make it so or give valid reasons why not. The contractor called one day when they were working on the kitchen cabinets. He said, "Cia there are five inches I can't account for."

Of course, he had changed Cia's design. He had put the dishwasher on the right side of the sink and Cia had put it on the left side. He also was not going to put a Lazy Susan in the corner.

When they talked it out and he redid the drawings, guess what, there was no five-inch discrepancy. He kept telling her, "Well if you want a Lazy Susie then you can have a lazy Susie." Cia chuckled remembering the encounter and how the contractor had named it lazy Susie instead of Susan.

The painter did not want to paint the outside of the house barn red like Cia's inspiration photo of the original house that was on display at the 1911 Illinois state fair. That house exactly like their renovated home. The painter also didn't like the trim color that Cia had picked out. Then she really got upset when Cia decided the fireplace needed to be something besides the brick. Someone had painted it with plaster mixed in and they could not clean it off to have the original brick to show and seal.

The painter got really upset and started screaming at Cia. When Cia walked into the house a few days later the trim color was not the same as the crown molding color. Cia asked and was told it was the same, it was just the way the light was hitting it. Well, the contractor came to the job site and the first thing out of his mouth was, "There are two different colors on the trims."

Cia said, "Finally someone other than me sees it. The painter's been trying to tell me it's the same." Although the paint can the painter used had the label stating it was the same color, it still didn't look right no matter how Cia looked at the trim and crown molding. Finally, Cia said, "I think perhaps, the crown molding had a better primer on it than what was put on the other trim."

She decided soon she would get some of the paint and try adding another coat to the trim and see if that helps. At that point, though, there was too much more to do than worry about the differences in the paint color.

CHAPTER 30

All Aboard!

Cia's children were not happy she was moving to Louisiana. Cia had felt used and not taken into consideration for much of her life, even with her children. She felt like she always had to take what was left over and pick up pieces for everyone else. None of her children thought about her at holiday times. Many had been spent alone.

They would even come to the town she lived in but never come to her house. If they did come, they came to drop off grandkids, leave, and go partying. Cia might have liked to be involved in the partying. Cia loved her grandkids and loved the times they got to spend together, but she longed for time with her children. Cia hoped they would make the effort to come and see her and her new home. She knew there was little chance they would, so she decided to do what she needed to do for herself. She had long ago tired of being there for everyone and only doing for others.

Cia's new home was her refuge and dream. She now had a chance to develop new friendships.

Cia also felt relief not having to take care of her mother. She loved her mother but the care she needed now, twenty-four hours a day, was more than Cia could do. Her own health--emotionally, physically, and psychologically--needed her to take care of herself. It all started with being true to herself. She knew she would visit her mother every time she could but determined to not feel guilty about moving away from Oklahoma. She had given almost thirty years to the care of her parents and felt she has done her fair share.

Cia was delighted with her new home and continued to think about the process of getting to this point. She realized she no longer had any siblings that were close in proximity to her. She was able to breathe and not have anyone judging her, at least to her face. They might be doing that behind her back, but she was relieved she was unaware of what anyone thought of her. She kept her siblings updated with pictures of what was going on. Some responded, others did not. Cia did not let that upset her. She was happy for the first time in her life.

The day Cia's baby grand piano was moved into her new home was a beautiful day. Jock made wedged pieces of wood to match the angle of the stairs and screwed plywood to the wedged pieces, so that they could smoothly roll the piano up the six steps of the front stairs leading into the house.

The new front door had side lights and one of the sidelights opened to give extra room for moving furniture in and out. It proved to be very beneficial in moving the piano into the house.

She was so excited to see it moved into the place she had saved especially for the baby grand piano. It perfectly fit and made the room a centerpiece of the whole home. She was disappointed she would have to wait, first for the piano guys to come and upright the piano, then wait some more for the piano tuner to come and tune the piano. There were adjustments that had to be made but it was finally tuned and ready to play.

Cia sat for over an hour playing on her piano. She felt a thrill of joy, the bright feelings that came over her and the beautiful music she created. She couldn't wait to play it for family and the new friends she had already made. She looked in awe at the way the piano fit perfectly into the space. Surrounded by all the other instruments, it looked absolutely perfect. You could see into the small bathroom with the wallpaper, and everything looked exactly as she'd dreamed it would.

As the days went by, Cia would walk by the piano, sit on the bench, play a tune or two. She always felt the joy of her home and the music she could play on her piano.

Cia knew she had reached her own nirvana. Her life was perfect. Jock was proud of the home they had created. He supported Cia in everything including her playing the piano. He always complemented the sound of her playing and was even getting his musical instruments down and playing more. He set up a stand on the back deck so he could practice and not disturb Cia while she wrote both in her diary and on her computer.

When Cia decided to write this book, tell her story, he was her champion encouraging her to write what she felt. He read the first part and gave a few critiques, not criticism but critiques. She'd learned there was a big difference. He said it was very good. He was an avid reader, reading every free moment he had. His remarks made Cia feel more confident in her writing.

After they were settled into their new home by November, they decided to try the Macedonia church that Jock had grown up in. Turned out, not only were the members of the church kind and welcoming but they were also in desperate need of a pianist. Cia felt very much at home in the church and decided this is what she had been looking for the past twelve years. She smiled and shook her head. "No, it was what I'd been seeking all my life."

Previously, they had tried several churches, but some were too small and not welcoming to new people, some were huge and didn't know new people were there, but this church was just right and wanted Cia and Jock to be a part of their congregation. Cia began to grow in her spiritual walk again and loved being in the church and accepted by more people. The ladies were welcoming and even talked about their home renovation and loved coming to visit. Cia felt she was finally home.

Jock's family were very welcoming and loved watching the

progress of the house being renovated. It felt awesome and Cia had lots of compliments and finally had a loving family to be a part of. Jock had a lot of cousins and aunts and uncles in the area. About two-thirds of the church he was related to at one level or another. It was great fun to see his classmates come and visit and tell stories of him during his school years. One of his classmates said he was always impressed with Jock but when he saw the things that Jock had created out of the doors and trim that was not reused in the house he was in total awe.

One of Cia's new friends bought twelve of the windows from the original house as well as the front door. She was very creative and made a greenhouse out of the windows and door. Cia felt like she was a part of it all and loved that the windows were getting used in such a lovely way.

Cia and Jock hosted their new neighbors for their first dinner party. Cia made chili and served it with Frito's. For dessert she had made some oatmeal, raisin with caramel bits cookies. It was Cia's favorite and the neighbors loved them also. Cia was finding great joy in cooking for others. One neighbor had knee surgery and was having a rough time with her mobility. When Cia made dinner for her and Jock she would make extra and share with the neighbors. They enjoyed the food and Cia got a great blessing helping them. Her neighbors come by at least two or three times a week and they love just sitting and visiting.

Cia and Jock made a quick trip to Oklahoma to pick up their trailer that had been in the shop fixing slide pulls that were damaged when they received it. They also picked up Candance since she would be out of school for a week, and it was Terrance's year to have her for Thanksgiving. Cia and Jock loved being with her as much as possible.

Cia and Jock also hosted Thanksgiving. Caleb and his family came on Tuesday of that week. Caleb told his mom that this was the prettiest house and homiest house that she had lived in. This made Cia very proud. Caleb and Cia spent the day in the kitchen while her daughter-in-law took the grandkids to the park. Cia was in heaven spending time with her son, just the two of them. It was healing for Cia. Then on Wednesday Cia's youngest brother and his wife and grandson came for Thanksgiving. Cia again cooked pies, pumpkin, and pecan, and made deviled eggs on Wednesday so she didn't have to be rushed on Thursday. She put the turkey and ham on to cook in the roasters and was able to sit and watch most of the Thanksgiving parade. Her brother and his family left on Friday noon and gave just enough time for Cia to catch her breath before having to take Candance back home to Norman.

    I *realize that my love for Jock is growing every day and that our marriage is stronger than it had ever been. Jock has the ability to help talk me down when my anxieties overwhelm me, and he has never been rude to me. I finally realize that he will never hurt me as I've been hurt in the past. I've been waiting for the other shoe to fall for years. I know it's not going to fall and I can relax and enjoy my golden years with my true love. All his friends and family stated that he's always been like that. I am excited for the next 11 years, or however much time the Lord allows us to have together. I feel that I have been truly blessed.*

Cia smiled as she rocked a little in her chair. She closed her diary and gave it a little pat. She picked up the diary, kissed the cover and said, "Thank you."

COPYRIGHT

This is a work of fiction. Names, characters, organizations, places, events, and incidents are either products of the author's imagination or are used fictitiously.

AUTHOR'S NOTES

My greatest wish for this book would be that someone will have the courage to stand up and leave an abusive situation. There is hope and there is someone who is looking for you.

My story is true to the best of my knowledge and my beliefs. I believe there is one God and that He alone is how you find peace. *He gives peace that passeth all understanding.* I have found when follow His direction that I prosper and life is much better. I try *not to lean on my own understanding* but look for guidance from Him.

The characters names have been changed to protect the innocent, or that don't agree with my recollection of my life. Most were not around 100% of the time, so they really never knew what I was going through. I'm thankful for those who were and were able to help lift me out of the mess I got myself into.

Made in the USA
Columbia, SC
26 May 2023

17292853R10085